NAOMI

ALIEN SURROGATE AGENCY #4

TASHA BLACK

13TH STORY PRESS

13th Story Press

PO Box 506

Swarthmore, PA 19081

13thStoryPress@gmail.com

Cover designed by Sylvia Frost of The Book Brander

TASHA BLACK STARTER LIBRARY

Packed with steamy shifters, mischievous magic, alien adventures, billionaire superheroes, and plenty of HEAT, the Tasha Black Starter Library is the perfect way to dive into Tasha's unique brand of Romance with Bite! Get your FREE books now at tashablack.com!

NAOMI

1

NAOMI

Naomi Peterson drank in the sights and scents of the idyllic meadow. Dew clung to the lush grass and a gentle breeze rustled fragrant pollen from the gorgeous purple wildflowers.

Or was that something else moving in the meadow?

She pricked her ears up and lifted her snout slightly, trying to taste prey on the air.

Nothing.

But maybe...

Coiling up tightly, she flattened herself the ground.

After a breathless moment of waiting and listening for clues, she released. Her borrowed body shot straight up into the air and curved downward to pounce, snout first, into the shivering flowers.

It had only been the breeze after all. She had stirred up nothing but a cloud of pollen.

But it felt so good to pounce that she did it several more times anyway, leaping madly around the meadow in big loops as the stretch of her muscles sent waves of endorphin-laced pleasure through her.

"*The scent of something refreshing wafts to you,*" a disembodied voice said calmly.

Naomi caught the scent. It was cool and sweet, an irresistible siren song of deliciousness.

"*Follow it, if you like,*" the voice said.

Abandoning the meadow, she picked her way through the deep grasses until she reached the shadow of the trees.

It was darker here, but her clever eyes adjusted immediately. She trotted into the woods, the soil cool and soft between her paws.

As the birdsong from the meadow faded, she chased down the trail of crystalline scent, her trot breaking into a series of leaps and bounds as her small heart raced with excitement.

"*Deep breaths, Naomi,*" Oberon's deep voice intoned calmly. "*Slow your heart rate.*"

Outside the simulation, Naomi closed her palms in her lap and opened them again very slowly, coaxing her breathing and heartbeat into slowing along with her hands.

When she first arrived at the Midsummer Fertility Center, Naomi had been so wound up that she'd had a hard time even sitting still. Hearing that her intended parent wasn't there yet and that she would have to cool her heels for an indefinite period of time was almost unbearable.

She had taken a few days to explore the Center's many incredible settings. It was hard to believe that the beach, the meadows, the lake, and the mountains had all been designed and created by an AI named Oberon.

It wasn't just that the spaces were beautiful. They each seemed to evoke an emotion in Naomi that was both sweet and... lonely. And the AI himself seemed more than happy to give her endless guided tours.

But even walking the grounds couldn't still her restlessness. Naomi had been working since she was a teenager. Relaxation wasn't really her thing.

And besides, she had left a career tangle behind that made her uncertain if she would even have a job when she went home again. A tangle so bad she might not be able to live the rest of her life without constantly looking over her shoulder.

Add to that her excitement and fear over her reason for being here, and it was impossible for her to find peace.

Naomi had always, *always* wanted to be a mother.

Her home planet of Terra-58 was known for being well-organized, peaceful, powerful, and prosperous. Many people credited the matriarchal society, which ensured that women held the highest governing positions, and that all wealth was passed through the maternal line.

A woman on Terra-58 who was ready for marriage and family would use a clinic to conceive her primary heir. After that child was born, she was eligible to marry and have as many more children as she liked with her husband.

Terra-58 was a paradise compared to the other Terras, with happy adults and beloved children - all of them, not just the primary heirs.

But for someone like Naomi, who struggled again and again to conceive at the clinics, it could mean an unjust life of terrible loneliness.

When a friend from the fertility feeds let her know about the top-secret Alien Fertility Agency and the option to act as an unconventional surrogate for a man from another world in exchange for the restoration of her own fertility, she hadn't been able to sign up fast enough.

Now that she was here, her mind and heart were constantly tugged between two extremes - fear about what was happening at her job back on Terra-58, and a wild, desperate hope that she might get to be a mother one day. Not even a long run on the beach was enough to calm her.

When Oberon suggested she enjoy a daily meditation, she almost laughed. If there was one thing Naomi had never been interested in, it was sitting still and thinking about nothing.

Though her friends described her as calm and elegant, it always made her feel like an imposter. Her professional demeanor was a carefully constructed facade for her active mind and restless spirit.

But there hadn't been anything else to take up her time and prevent her from trying something new. And after so many tense and endless days, she was beginning to think that Oberon might have a point.

She might need to take advantage of a chance to relax.

So, she'd agreed to try one of his meditation programs. On the first morning, she had barely been able to clear her mind for two minutes.

Oberon began suggesting that she picture various natural settings. From her long walks and explorations, he had rightly gleaned that she loved nature.

But it wasn't until he suggested picturing animals that Naomi turned a corner and was able to sink deep, deep into her inner peace.

It was probably unusual to picture *herself* as the animal. But the whole idea of meditation was a little silly to her anyway. Did it really matter how far out of her usual comfort zone she went?

And besides, who was going to judge her for it?

She had been alone at the Center for weeks without a match.

And now she was distracted, as usual.

In her mind, she returned to her fox form and followed the sweet scent trail all the way to its origin.

Light was filtering through the trees, warming her soft fur, and showing her the glittering, glassy surface of the burbling creek whose scent had drawn her here.

An expanse of smooth stone jutted out over the water, and she trotted out onto it, enjoying the feel of the sun warmed surface under her paws. When she reached the end of the stone, she leaned forward to peer into the water.

At first, she saw her human reflection gazing back at her through a curtain of long, dark hair.

Before her eyes, it faded and sharpened into the adorable furry face of a Terran fox - large, dark eyes in a pale orange face, framed by even larger ears with black pointed tips.

Naomi had seen one in a holo-film once, and fallen in love with the oddly serious-yet-silly beasts. When Oberon asked her to picture an animal, this little creature had pounced into her mind.

She lowered herself onto her belly, getting just close enough to the water to dip her snout in and take a long, satisfying pull.

The water cascaded down her throat, cool and sweet.

"Time to ease out of your meditation, Naomi," Oberon murmured to her. *"A guest is arriving at the Center for you."*

Normally, winding down her meditation session was slow and relaxing, and Naomi managed to carry her sense of calm into the next few hours of her day.

But the news of a visitor sent a chill down her spine, and she felt her stomach tighten so much she regretted eating breakfast. Panic sent ice water through her veins and it felt suddenly as if she had never meditated at all.

"Do you know anything about this guest?" she asked Oberon as calmly as she could.

"It is your prospective parent, Naomi," Oberon said. "Apologies for not being clear. The Center discourages visitors who are not part of the program."

Discourages...

That was relieving, though *prohibits* would have been better, safer.

Oddly though, she was still feeling panicky. Meeting the prospective parent suddenly seemed even more nerve-racking than facing the firm.

What if he didn't like her and just walked away?

What if they weren't compatible after all?

"Do not fear, Naomi," Oberon said. "No harm will come to you from the prospective parent."

She had momentarily forgotten the AI could read her vital signs.

Naomi opened her eyes and stretched slowly, trying to force her heartbeat back to normal.

"You have approximately fourteen minutes, if there is anything you wish to do to ready yourself before the meeting," Oberon said.

"Thank you," Naomi said, standing and brushing off her tights. "I'll just take a quick shower and get changed."

"Excellent," Oberon said.

A door appeared in the corner of the all-white room, and she took a deep breath, trying to compose herself before heading to it.

2

GAGE

age Zeyr'n stood at the threshold of the shuttle ship, fighting back his impatience as a butler droid fussed with his tie.

It hummed lightly as it rolled side to side in front of him, tightening the silken noose and straightening it, and then tightening it all over again.

The custom-tailored suit and Drathian silk tie were gifts from his employers, their value probably greater than a year of Gage's normal compensation.

But they paled in comparison to the larger gifts.

The first was an extremely early retirement, with full pay and benefits for life - all backed by a trust in his name, in case anything ever happened to them.

The second was the title to a stone carriage house with a big vegetable garden and a meadow for his canine partner to run in, carved from their own estate.

And the third, and most expensive gift of all, was this trip to the Midsummer Fertility Center.

While any lucky Maltaffian guard might receive early pension for an exceptional job, or save up for a house of his own one day, this unique access to an off-planet surrogate to conceive and bear an heir was an unheard-of luxury, reserved for only the wealthiest on the planet.

Gage had tried to refuse it. In his eyes it was too much.

It was all too much, really. He had only been doing his job.

But the Bly-Xarxyn family had insisted. Gage had saved their children from a kidnapper's plot. They were determined to repay him somehow.

"The only fair reward for you protecting our family is for us to give you the opportunity to enjoy a family of your own, my good man," Dayvees Bly-Xarxyn told him merrily while sucking on a Vystian cigar.

"I don't need an heir," Gage had replied gruffly.

"Of course you do," Dayvees laughed. "You have a pension and property now. Besides, I hear some of these surrogates are tender little Terrans." He gave a chef's kiss and winked at Gage.

"Dayvees," his wife, Emyra scolded playfully. "You'll embarrass him."

"It would take more than that, madam," Gage said.

But he was lying. It took all his training not to let the blood rush to his cheeks. Living on duty these last years had taken its toll. He hadn't been with a woman in so long...

"Call me Emyra," she said, scolding him now, instead of her husband. "We're family friends now. We're not your employers anymore."

He smiled at her indulgently. She was a kind lady, and her husband was a good man. But Gage would never be one of them. The elite of Maltaffia practically spoke their own language. Living among them for so long had taught him their ways, but it just wasn't in his blood.

And he didn't like the sense of obligation that accepting their gifts conferred on him.

Besides, who was he if he wasn't a Maltaffian guard? All Maltaffian men completed the required training, but Gage had taken the bonds, pledging to put his clients before himself for life.

Now, he felt unmoored and restless.

The droid in front of him beeped and let out a low whistle.

The clear glass window in front of him darkened momentarily to show him his reflection.

The usual Maltaffian's guard's garb was straightforward and down to business. It didn't pretend to be anything but exactly what it was.

But the man staring back at him in the glass was swathed in the most luxurious fabric, tailored perfectly to his wide shoulders. He appeared to be sophisticated and wealthy, confident and self-assured.

A warm snout at his crotch reminded him who he really was.

"Athena," he reprimanded his partner.

Normally, the Firmament Shepherd was one hundred percent professional, one hundred percent of the time. But since their retirement, she had been a little irritable.

Half the time, he encouraged her to be playful and enjoy herself. The other half, he just tried not to grind his teeth as he watched her pace and whine at the closet door, asking for her officer's vest.

And there was no way to tell her she would never wear it again.

He'd had to bite his tongue when the Bly-Xarxyns told him they were bringing in a fresh Maltaffian guard with a canine partner to take his place.

He might feel a little, or even a lot, uncomfortable watching the new guard work. But Athena would be *heartbroken* that another officer was walking *her* charges to the hovercar and keeping watch over their games in the gardens.

Athena snuffled at the suit again, three inward sniffs and one huff out, as if to clear her nose of the unpleasant new smell.

"It's just for a week," he told her. "It won't be that bad."

He wasn't entirely sure which one of them he was trying to convince.

The door hissed as the seal unlocked, and Gage walked down the ramp onto a sandy beach.

Athena moved briskly to his side, all concerns about his wardrobe forgotten. Officer's vest or no, she had not forgotten her duties. They were entering a new place, and precautions had to be taken.

To the north of the craft, the waters of a cerulean blue ocean frothed and waved. East and west, the pale gold sand of the beach stretched in both directions as far as the eye could see.

Annoyingly, the land on the other side of the craft was completely blocked by the craft itself, which could have easily turned to block the ocean view instead, allowing Gage to see the inhabited part of the Center.

For all he knew, there could be a thousand Armada soldiers lined up on the other side of the craft. Or it could be nothing but unoccupied miles of beach and inland. But Gage could prepare for neither, since he couldn't fracking see.

"They probably designed it to impress people with the ocean view," he told Athena, rolling his eyes. "Not a single thought for security. Literally anything could be waiting for us on the other side of this vessel."

Athena huffed out a backward sniff in agreement. Though she couldn't understand his words, she knew they were not supposed to expose themselves unnecessarily in a new place.

At least for Gage, there was no client to protect. But Athena didn't really know she was supposed to be off duty.

"Together," he told her firmly when he saw her try to slink past him and get the first look at what they were up against.

She straightened and waited for him, ears pricked up.

They stuck to the side of the craft and scanned the beach carefully, bit by bit, as they came around the corner to find that the craft had been blocking two things.

Directly behind it was a tiki bar that looked like something out of the musical holo-films. It appeared to be well-stocked with dozens of colorful bottles and an array of glassware hanging on hooks from the ceiling. But there was no attendant in sight, and no one sat at the rattan bar.

To the right of the tiki bar was a path of flat stones leading between the coconut trees and away from the water.

He scanned left and right again, but there was no one on the beach to greet him.

"No point sitting around the bar," he told Athena. "Let's go."

They headed to the path together, feet and paws sinking in the sun-warmed sand until they reached the stones.

Gage found himself relaxing slightly - probably the effect of the fresh air and pleasant weather. When he was guarding, he spent some time outdoors on patrol, but for the most part, the Bly-Xarxyns were indoor people.

He was secretly very pleased about that vegetable patch

that was waiting for him when he was done here. The outdoors agreed with him. That was one aspect of retirement he wouldn't resent.

"You'll like it better outside too, Athena," he told her. "You have been very professional all your life, but a dog should have her feet in the mud from time to time. You'll see."

Athena didn't answer, of course, but her ears flicked. She was listening.

More and more grass poked up through the sand as they traveled, until they were finally walking through a meadow of wildflowers instead of a beach.

The stones continued through the meadow, and Gage shook his head when he observed that the meadow was tree-lined on three sides. Why would they be sent directly down the middle, with no cover whatsoever?

Butterflies flitted among the blossoms, but they couldn't offer him answers.

Athena snuffled once when a butterfly came close to landing on her snout. Otherwise, she trotted along calmly.

Gage trusted her superior senses. If something here was not as it should be, Athena would alert him.

They followed the path into the cool shade of the woods and along a looping, hilly trail that finally let out in what looked a lot like the countryside where Gage had grown up.

He had loved the beautiful fields of grain and leafy spine flower. The farm was a magical place to grow up.

When his sister wanted to go to school for healing, his parents decided to sell the farm and move to a small apartment in the city. They accepted a bid from a couple with a familiar sounding last name.

But those people were just a front for a major corporation.

The contract was assigned to CosmicChem before settlement, and before they knew it, his family had unknowingly sold yet another farm to be dismantled and rezoned.

It was one thing to choose to sell to a faceless giant like CosmicChem with one's eyes open, to get a superior price, like many families before them had done.

But to be tricked into selling to them against your will?

Gage's father had been heartbroken. They had never had the heart to even drive down that street when they visited their hometown.

It was for this reason that Gage himself had chosen a residential guard job rather than a higher paid position with a big franchise. The Bly-Xarxyns might be rich and eccentric, but they were at least decent beings, who didn't make their money by exploiting people.

The path curved slightly and revealed a small hillside with a big farmhouse halfway up. A vegetable garden covered the hill below, and the path of stones wound up to the front door.

"Wow," he murmured.

He had heard that the Center could transform itself to make the space more pleasurable for its occupants.

Naturally, he had imagined that in terms of sexual things, strange furniture or kinky items appearing out of nowhere.

It never occurred to him that the Center would transform itself to make him feel *at home*.

"I'm probably overthinking it," he told Athena. "I bet there's always a farmhouse here. Everyone likes a farmhouse."

Athena just kept walking, in perfect synch with his footsteps. When she was focused on her job, she didn't indulge his idle chitchat.

When he knocked on the door, it opened for him, revealing that the interior of the house to be a small, bistro-type restaurant.

He swept the space with his eyes, realizing immediately that this was much better than the beach.

There were tables set against walls, and mirrors at sensible intervals to reveal the hidden corners. Though the back of the house had huge windows with a view of the hillside above, there were only two doors leading outside, and he could see them both from the tables, if he kept his back to the wall.

He stepped in, with Athena by his side, bracing himself for the inevitable demand for her papers.

As a Maltaffian Canine Officer, First Class, Athena was entitled to all the privileges her position conferred, even post-retirement.

But no one accosted him, and he realized that of course, this whole thing was manufactured just for him and his intended surrogate. There would be no other customers, and the AI who designed the space had to know about the dog.

He strode over to an ideal table with an easy view of all egresses, and sat with his back to the wall.

Athena settled in beside him, leaning the warm weight of her shoulder against his thigh in her usual way, so that he could be sure of her without glancing down.

This was not something she had been trained to do. Gage liked to think it was her expression of their special bond.

"Good work, Athena," he told her.

Her thick tail whacked once against his chair.

Then he leaned back, and they waited together for whatever the Center wanted from them next.

Just as he sank into the golden peace of the calm watchfulness that sustained him during long periods on duty, the back door to the bistro opened.

A woman with long, dark hair stepped inside. She was tall for a Terran, her soft features set in a serious expression.

She moved inside, blinking twice, presumably to adjust her eyes to dim lighting after the warm sunlight outside.

Something about the way she carried herself seemed to crack a stone wall he hadn't known was in his chest, leaving him breathless.

There was no room in his mind anymore for the uncomfortable tie, the security sweeps, or even his memories of the old farm.

There was only the woman.

And she was turning her head and about to notice him.

3

NAOMI

aomi stepped into the farmhouse, blinking away the transition from bright sunshine to the softly lit interior.

But it wasn't a farmhouse, really. It was set up like an upscale café, and she guessed it was most likely a charming farm-to-table affair, based on the setting.

She relaxed a little. Her work had put her in a dozen little places like this for lunch meetings with clients. It even smelled familiar, like fresh bread and simmering garlic.

She felt a bit more at home than she had a moment ago.

Scanning the space, she noticed a man in a very expensive suit at a table by the wall was the only other occupant. His skin was a pale green, and his head was adorned with a glorious pair of horns sprouting out of a mane of silky hair.

Maltaffian.

She tried desperately to remember whether Maltaffians had to actually mate to conceive a child, but drew a blank.

He was looking at her, an odd expression on his annoyingly handsome face, and he stood to greet her, almost like he heard distant music and was trying to remember the composer's name.

Though she had no particular interest in high end fashion herself, she recognized the bespoke fit of his clothing the instant he stood. And that tie had to be Drathian silk.

The awful lawyers at her firm were always bragging about what they were wearing, and yelling out the prices, as if anyone should be impressed that they spent so much on a tie they could have chosen to feed a shelter of hungry families or retrofit an entire school library on one of the lower Terras and still had enough change left over for a closetful of equally ugly ties.

Don't judge. This outrageously rich snob is the reason you're here, the reason you might be able to conceive a child of your own one day.

"Hello," she said politely. "I'm Naomi, the prospective surrogate."

As she got closer, she saw that he wasn't alone. A gigantic canine sat by his side, its ears pricked up with interest.

Naomi's heart melted immediately as she took in the shaggy, cloud-gray pelt and large, brown eyes.

"Oh," she said softly, crouching down and extending her open palms. "Hello, there."

A growl so low it sounded like a freight-hover emitted from the furry muzzle.

That was odd. Naomi was great with animals. She loved them, and they loved her. Or at least they did until now. The only reason she didn't have a pet of her own was her relentless work schedule.

"He's beautiful," she said, straightening up and

addressing the man instead, so as to give the canine a moment to accustom itself to her.

"Her name is Athena," the man said.

She expected him to say more, but he just kept staring at her with that strange, dreamy expression, like she was about to hand him the winning numbers to the sector lotto.

Glancing back down at the dog, she had to fight the instinct to apologize for guessing its gender wrong.

"Hello, Athena," she said softly instead.

If she was waiting for a thump of its tail, the wait was clearly going to be in vain. The dog didn't even blink at her.

"It's a pleasure to meet you," the man said at last, almost startling her. "Gage."

His voice was even deeper than Athena's growl, something about it made her a little weak in the knees. And he still wore that expression - so soft for such a huge, muscular man. Even the harsh planes of his face defied the haze in his eyes as he drank her in like he was dying of thirst.

Suddenly, Naomi was aware of the way her dress wrapped around her ribs, the air in the room swirling on her skin, her own heartbeat throbbing in her chest.

"Hello, there, I'm Dr. Oppyx," a bright, cheerful voice came from the front door. "I see you two have met."

"We three," Naomi said, tearing her eyes from Gage to greet the new arrival.

"Ah, yes," a small Maltaffian woman in a lab coat said warmly. "Athena is with us too. Oberon has taken great pains to ensure she enjoys her stay, Gage. But if you notice anything we can do to improve, please let us know. She is our first canine guest."

"Thank you very much," he replied respectfully.

Naomi tried to hide her surprise. In her experience, a

man of Gage's position would be trying to assert himself and demand more at any opportunity.

Instead, he was friendly and down to earth, and it was his dog who acted like she was too good for this place.

Naomi stole another glance at her, just in case she had relaxed, but the beautiful gray canine was staring straight ahead, shoulders back, snout perfectly parallel with the floor, like she was posing for a marble statue.

"Why don't the two of you have a seat, so we can begin the holo-film welcoming you to the Center?" Dr. Oppyx offered, gesturing to a small couch in the waiting area of the café.

The sofa hardly looked large enough for just Gage, but Naomi marched over anyway. If she knew one thing about men of means, it was that you did what they wanted and let them complain if something wasn't right.

She squeezed herself as far to the side as possible.

Gage joined her, lowering himself gingerly onto the cushions.

His big thigh pressed against hers, sending more ripples of awareness through her.

"Excellent," Dr. Oppyx announced.

But then Athena was snuffling and snaking her snout between them, almost as if she was trying to nudge Naomi off the sofa.

"Athena, my other side," Gage said, jerking his chin the other way.

The dog huffed out a sniff and moved to sit beside the sofa.

"Sorry," he said. "She's used to being on my right."

"Should we switch places?" Naomi offered.

"No, no, it's fine," Gage said with a tight smile.

"Very well," Dr. Oppyx said.

The lights dimmed so that Naomi was aware only of the big, hard body beside hers, and the excited thrum of her own heartbeat.

4

GAGE

Gage tried desperately to focus on the doctor, who was fussing with a holo projector on a nearby table.

But all he could think about was the delicious little beauty beside him. Her every movement unleashed a breath of her scent, each one driving him closer to madness.

What's happening to me?

But he knew what was happening. He wanted the cool-headed little Terran, wanted her badly.

And he had no one to blame but himself. It had been years since he had indulged in a little time on the pleasure ships, let alone had a woman in his bed that he had wooed and won.

Now, at the slightest suggestion that he was going to engage in a mating with this stranger, he was as rigid with need as a frantic teenager.

He could only beg the gods that she kept her professional composure, and her eyes didn't drift below his face. She would probably find his physical reaction to her shocking, maybe even frightening, given her tiny frame and the burgeoning swell of his need.

A flickering image appeared over the holo-disc the doctor was fussing with. As Dr. Oppyx stepped back into the shadows, Gage forced his eyes to focus on the film.

It appeared to be a female Maltaffian. She was walking on the same beach where his shuttle craft had arrived.

"Welcome to the Midsummer Center for Fertility," the woman said in a cheerful tone. "I'm here to tell you a little about the center and the work we'll be doing here. Let me start by saying that you are the most important part of that work."

The view panned out slightly, showing more of the beach.

"A first of its kind, the entire center was uniquely designed, planned and implemented by a single AI," she said as she walked. "And that AI, nicknamed Oberon, will also host you throughout your stay, attending to all of your needs and ensuring the best possible environment to meet our goals. We're proud to tell you that the Midsummer Center for Fertility was denoted by the Intergalactic Physicians Association as the most conception-friendly place in the galaxy."

The woman turned, and suddenly she was in a green meadow. The sound of birdsong swelled around her.

"Each day will begin with relaxing, shared activities for surrogate and intended parent," the woman went on. "Oberon has crafted a plethora of pleasant locations to help you feel at ease and get to know each other better."

That was good. No matter what was happening to his libido in the presence of this girl, Gage knew that his sperm would not quicken until he had formed a bond with her. Time together would encourage success.

His mind showed him images of how they could spend that time. He saw her spread out on his bed, his big green hands holding her pale thighs down, feeding on her needy sex while she tossed her dark hair against the pillows, moaning and begging for more.

He barely held back a groan of wanting.

"Here at the Midsummer Center for Fertility, everyone has responsibilities," the woman said, her voice deepening as if she had also seen his fantasy, and did not approve.

The camera zoomed in on her face in a dramatic close-up.

"It's the responsibility of this clinic to ensure your safety at all times," she said. "Say the words *escape me now* at any time, and Oberon will cancel programming immediately."

He glanced over at Naomi, wondering what she made of all this. Would she ask Oberon to take her away from him if he let her see that he wanted to do so much more than spill his seed in her?

He could practically hear her desperate cries as he pleasured her over and over again.

What was wrong with him?

She tilted her chin up and studied his face, her lips parted slightly, as if she could hear his thoughts.

"In addition, for security and training purposes, everything that happens at the Midsummer Center for Fertility will be recorded," the woman went on. "However, if you say the words *confirm privacy mode*, Oberon will not record or display the proceedings to our staff."

But the words were merely washing over him now. He couldn't absorb anything else with her eyes on him.

He dragged his eyes back to the film, clenching the arm of the sofa until he was afraid it would buckle, barely holding himself back from touching her.

"It is the responsibility of the surrogate to submit to the necessary procedures to accomplish a pregnancy," the woman said brightly. "As a side note, according to our exit polls, 95% of participants find the procedure to be highly to extremely enjoyable."

Gods, but he would make her scream with rapture.

He could feel the tension in her from the places where their bodies touched. She was as tight as the strings on a vibroharp, and he would make her sing.

"Upon successful conception, the surrogate will protect herself and the developing fetus by any means necessary to ensure a healthy birth," the woman was saying. "We will do all we can to ensure that the surrogate's experience is a pleasant one. However, the surrogate understands that her experience here is unique to the program. At the end of the gestational period, she will return to her home planet, and there will be no further contact with the father or the offspring."

Gage's reaction was furious and visceral.

He hadn't come here looking for a girlfriend, but the idea that this Terran would be allowed to accept him and then trot off again to her home planet, never to see him again, was unacceptable.

Mine.

His heart stuttered in his chest. That word. It had come out of nowhere. He had not summoned it, or even considered the possibility.

Could this Terran woman be his true mate?

"It is the responsibility of the prospective parent to treat the surrogate with respect," the woman on the holo-film went on in the background of his thoughts. "Abuse of any kind will not be tolerated. Renewed consent is required for each act of physical intimacy."

But there could be no fear of abuse if he was her true mate. There would only be endless pleasure and longing between them.

He closed his eyes against the flames of desire the thought ignited in him, praying for the strength to make it through this presentation, until he could get her alone and find out the truth of his feelings, and hers.

5

NAOMI

Naomi took slow, calming breaths and resisted the impulse to squirm in her seat beside the big alien.

Barely.

His hard thigh felt so good against hers, and heat seemed to pour out of him, warming her and sending little ripples of awareness down her spine.

Best of all was his clean, masculine scent. She longed to press her nose to his chest and drink it in.

"Do either of you have any questions?" Dr. Oppyx asked brightly, as the lights came back on.

None that I can ask out loud...

Naomi bit her lip and hoped the heat in her cheeks wasn't turning her face bright red. She had pretty much stopped listening once it became clear that yes, Maltaffians *did* need a physical mating experience to bring their seed to life.

"None?" Dr. Oppyx asked.

"It all seemed similar to the information in the contract," Naomi guessed.

"Yes," Dr. Oppyx said, smiling. "Well, if you two are all set, then it's time for your first bonding activity together."

Gage nodded to her.

"Very well," Dr. Oppyx said. "You're going to head out the back door and turn right through the trellis. When you reach the end of the trail, your dinner will be waiting for you."

"Thank you," Naomi said, standing and stepping a bit away from the sofa to give Gage room to stand.

As soon as he did, Athena was between them again, as if she had teleported. Her stance was relaxed, but her ears pricked up expectantly.

It was probably just the light, but to Naomi, her cloudy-gray fur looked darker now, almost rain-cloudy.

The three of them moved together toward the back door, where Naomi had come in. It opened on its own, letting in a breath of delicious country air.

Naomi jogged down the steps and headed to the right, where a massive wooden trellis hung with blossoming roses formed a gate between the hedges.

She turned back to see that Gage was right behind her, with Athena at his side.

"We'll go first," he told her. "If you don't mind."

"Of course not," she said curiously.

He approached the trellis like a gentleman spy in a holo-film, with a wary confidence.

"Athena," he said.

The dog darted through the trellis and barked once.

It was one of the oddest barks Naomi had ever heard. It sounded as if the dog was saying *bark* and nothing more. It was as if she did not like the sound of her own barking, and was releasing the least possible amount of sound to get the job done.

It must have meant something to Gage, since he gestured for Naomi to follow him as he stepped through the trellis.

"Interesting," he said.

As soon as she joined him on the other side, her breath caught in her throat.

The farm and the farmhouse were gone, replaced by a towering forest. Massive trees stretched up from thick, mossy trunks, their branches snagging on the low-hanging clouds above.

A humid mist clung to the ground, making the greens and browns of the moss and mushrooms seem even darker and more lush.

"Incredible," she breathed.

"I know that all of this was created for us," Gage said slowly. "But it's so real that it keeps taking me by surprise."

"And you've only been here a few minutes," Naomi said dryly, starting off down the path.

"What do you mean?" he asked.

He held up a vine so that she could walk under it, and she almost felt bad for her remark.

"I've been here a bit longer than you," she said lightly. "That's all."

"How long have you been here?" he asked.

"It all started to blend together after the first week," she said, winking at him.

"*Rings of the Outer Realms*," he muttered to himself.

"What?" she asked.

"They knew," he said, shaking his head. "They knew all along."

"They knew what?" she demanded. "Who knew?"

He glanced down at her as if just remembering that she existed.

Suddenly, his face went blank.

"Gage?" she asked. "What's going on?"

"Oh, nothing," he told her. "To be completely honest, I had some doubts about this. But it sounds like the Center assumed I would come anyway."

Her horrified reaction must have shown on her face.

"I want a baby," he told her immediately. "That's not a question. I've always wanted a family, please don't be afraid that a child we conceived wouldn't be loved and wanted."

"I wasn't," she lied.

While the men of Terra-58 were all desperate for marriage and family, she had heard that men on other worlds were more cavalier.

For the gender with less power, an allegiance with a family unit might offer safety and security. And for the other, a responsibility and a loss of freedoms.

Was Gage such a man?

And if he was, why would he pay a fortune to come here and have a child?

"Friends of mine helped me arrange this," he told her. "I wasn't sure about the timing with my work, that's all. But when the Center let them know you were a match, they must have said yes before confirming with me. They thought you were quite a genetic catch."

"Uh, thanks," she said. "So, your work is demanding?"

"It won't be after this," he said, smiling warmly at her. "I expect to have my hands full with home responsibilities."

She tried to picture him with a tiny baby, and somehow it was the easiest thing in the world, in spite of the fancy suit and his massive size. She could just picture the little one, held snug to his wide chest, reaching for the slender golden chains that hung from his horns.

As if to make it easier for her, he chose that moment to

shrug off his jacket and hold it over his shoulder. His wide frame tested the tensile strength of the white algodon of his button-down shirt.

With superhuman resolve, she tore her eyes from his big body and focused on the path ahead.

"Oh no," she breathed, seeing what was coming.

"What's wrong?" he asked.

But she was so overcome that she couldn't find any words.

Just ahead, the trail opened onto a narrow bridge, suspended over the forest below. Nearly invisible wires held up a floor made of a thin, metal grate.

As she studied it in horror, the wind picked up slightly and the whole thing *moved.*

"Is it the bridge?" he asked her gently.

"I... I can't," she murmured.

"You're afraid of heights?" he guessed.

She nodded.

"We'll just turn around and ask Dr. Oppyx if there's another way to get where we're going," he told her.

She smiled up at him gratefully, but he was looking over her shoulder with a horrified expression.

She turned to see what he was looking at and her heart sank.

The forest had closed up behind them, leaving no open path, and nothing to indicate how to get back to the farmhouse.

"This must be Oberon encouraging me to push through my comfort zone," she said resigning herself.

"He would do that?" Gage asked, looking surprised.

"Everything here is by design," she told him. "Everything."

"He knows you're afraid of heights?" Gage asked.

She thought back to the week she had spent at the Center, wondering if she had offered that info at any point.

"He probably extrapolated it from the activities I chose to partake in and the ones I didn't," she realized out loud.

"Why would he want to scare you now?" Gage asked, a furrow appearing on his perfect brow.

She pushed down the wild impulse that told her to kiss it away.

"He wants us to bond," she said. "He wants you to help me get across the bridge."

The bridge creaked, as if in agreement, and they both turned back to it.

This time, Naomi tried to focus on the other side of the bridge, where the path picked up again. She could *see* the cool, modern-looking house where their dinner was probably waiting. Warm light glowed in all the windows.

"It's not that far," she ventured.

Athena, who had reached the end of the bridge long before, barked once, as if to remind them they had places to be.

"I guess she wants her dinner, too," Naomi joked weakly.

"We'll take it one step at a time," Gage told her, his voice calm and slow. "Try to keep your focus on the other side of the bridge."

She nodded once and stepped forward, willing herself not to think about anything but her destination, where her dinner awaited.

When you get there, you get more than dinner.

Fear and desire swirled in her belly, making her feel almost dizzy, and she hadn't set one foot on the bridge yet.

"Where do you want me?" Gage asked her, his steady voice an anchor in her sea of emotion.

"Behind me, maybe?" she suggested. "And Athena in front."

"We can definitely do that," he told her. "Athena, let's go."

The dog trotted casually out onto the bridge as if she spent half her life precariously standing over a mountain-height chasm.

Naomi took a deep breath and followed.

Don't look down, don't look at the grate.

She fixed her eyes on the far end of the bridge and the warm, yellow light in the windows of the house.

Her shoes clanked on the metal, and she nearly looked down, but managed to stay focused.

She could feel the breeze even here on the edge of the bridge. She would probably feel it coming up from underneath too once they were out in the middle.

"You okay?" Gage asked from behind her.

"Fine," she managed.

His feet hit the bridge, and she felt it sway slightly as it took his weight.

She closed her eyes.

"We can ask Oberon to stop the program," Gage murmured. "I'm sure it happens all the time."

"No," she said. "No, we can't fail on our first mission. I've got this."

She opened her eyes and took another step forward, and then another.

Gage began to move too, and the bridge swayed with his weight.

Her stomach lurched and she clung to the rails along the side, fighting the urge to retch.

"What's happening, Naomi? Talk to me," Gage said sternly.

"When it moves, I..." she struggled to find the words. "It feels like we're falling."

"Okay," he said. "Okay, so we have to move together, then you won't notice it. If I step when you step, but on the opposite side, it won't sway."

"That's a good idea," she said, surprised. "Do we count, or what?"

"Yes," he said. "Let's count. Ready?"

She was not ready. She would never be ready. All she wanted was to turn around, push him out of the way, and run back to solid ground.

But more than she wanted that, she wanted a baby.

"Okay, on three," she said. "One, two, three."

She stepped forward on her right foot on three and Gage must have timed his left step perfectly, because she felt nothing.

But they were off rhythm for the next step, and when the bridge lurched, she felt the twist of her stomach almost up to her chest.

"How about a song?" Gage suggested. "To keep us in step? Name a song you like."

"*Heated Dreams*," she said automatically, without thinking about how embarrassing it was that she still listened to girl bands.

"*Heated Dreams* by the Feral Kittens?" Gage asked, sounding amazed.

"It's catchy," Naomi said weakly.

"No, no, it's fantastic," Gage said. "But you might have to remind me of the words."

Naomi closed her eyes and started singing, stepping on every down beat.

Gage chuckled behind her as they went, marching along with her.

The song was a real banger, about a woman who was in love with her best friend but afraid to tell him. She kept trying to get up her nerve to talk to him, but every time she did, she woke up afterward, having only made her move in her dreams.

As the song went on, the woman grew more and more wanton in her attempts to win over the guy, until at last she was practically making love to him in her dreams, and then waking up to nothing.

By the time they were halfway across the bridge, Gage was singing along with the chorus.

"*Heated, heated, heated, heated dreeeeeeams, babyyyyyy,*" he sang out in his booming voice.

The sound echoed off the cliffside Naomi was actively trying to forget was beneath them, and she shivered with fear, even as her cheeks ached from smiling at the way the big man threw himself into the song.

They were nearly across when Athena spotted something in the trees.

The massive canine let out a bark as loud as a gunshot and took off, her leaps causing the bridge to swing wildly.

Naomi stumbled slightly, bracing herself against the side, and finally making the mistake of allowing her eyes to drop to the grate below.

She was looking down into the tops of trees, so far below her that they looked almost like the broccoli section at the veggie stand.

Clouds moved all around her, even *below* her feet.

Panic clenched her heart like a fist, and the edges of her vision went dark.

Then big, warm arms were wrapping around her, and she was being lifted.

"I've got you," Gage murmured into her hair as he pulled her into his chest.

She clung to him, her eyes squeezed shut. Surely, it was worse to be held up high, too high for the sides of the bridge to hold her in.

But being anywhere but his arms seemed beyond terrifying.

"Hurry," she whispered against his chest.

Then he was running, singing the words to the song all wrong, as if he might distract her.

She wanted to laugh, but she was too scared to take in a whole breath. Instead, she tried to focus on the delicious scent of him, and the warmth of his muscles as they bunched and flexed against her with every rhythmic step.

6

GAGE

Gage moved as quickly as he dared, cradling Naomi to his chest.

He was worried about her, but since the bridge was sturdy, and he knew they would be fine, he was also able to worry about what was making Athena bark.

The big canine wasn't one to send up a false alarm. If she was worried, there was something to worry about.

And he had to face whatever it was with a soft, frightened Terran in his arms, blurring his senses with her sweet fragrance.

At last, his feet hit solid ground.

"Thank the stars," Naomi murmured, using one of his grandmother's favorite phrases.

She made a move as if she was going to get down.

"Hold still," he instructed her. "Athena, what's wrong?"

The dog turned to him, her whole body stiff as a board and quivering.

"My apologies, Gage," a disembodied voice said. "One of our staff was laying out your meal."

"Oberon?" he guessed.

"Yes, sir," the voice replied. "I will bear in mind that Athena should meet more of the staff, so that we do not trouble her further."

Gage figured Athena would always be troubled at someone in his space unexpectedly, whether she had *met* them or not. But he chose to be polite. After all, this wasn't his home.

"Thank you," he said instead. "We'll head in then."

But he paused right where he was. Now that he knew all was well inside, his whole focus was on the woman in his arms.

Whatever was happening between them, he felt her fear and pain as if they were her own.

And what she felt right now was shame.

"Would you like me to place you down now?" he asked, wondering if having her autonomy would make her feel better.

She nodded against his chest, still clinging to him, as if her nod had been untrue.

"Shall I carry you just as far as the house?" he offered.

"No," she whispered. "No, I'll be fine."

She wiggled a bit, and he let her slide slowly down his body.

The movement set his own senses on fire, and he prayed she would not be offended at the obvious evidence of his desire.

This is why we are here, to mate and conceive a child.

It still seemed inappropriate to desire her so terribly when she was so scared.

She tilted her head up to meet his eyes. Hers were large, the deepest chocolate brown in color, and slightly hazy, as if she felt it too, the pull between them.

"Let's go in," he said, clearing his throat.

It was the most natural thing in the world to wrap his hand around hers as they headed up the steps to the house.

"Put your hand on the sensor," he suggested.

She placed her free palm against the glass, and the door slid open instantly to reveal a modern-style mountain house.

The living space was all open, with a crackling fire beside the big dining table.

"Wow," she murmured. "It's like something out of the holo-films."

She dashed off to the door that must be the bedroom, and his excitement only grew at the thought of what they would be doing in there.

"It's *enormous*," she called back to him.

You have no idea...

He glanced past her into a room that seemed like most other bedrooms to him. It hit Gage suddenly that inadvertently living along with his employers' lifestyle for so many years had spoiled him.

The house *was* incredible. And the view over the forest was exquisite.

Nearly as exquisite as Naomi's awestruck smile as she walked back to join him.

"I guess this is no big deal for you," she said, her expression turning wry and teasing.

"It's beautiful," he said, not taking his eyes off her. "This is definitely a big deal."

The air seemed to go out of the room as he realized that he was talking about more than just the view. He was talking about the time they would spend together, and the purpose of their visit.

And unbeknownst to Naomi, he was also thinking of his intense attraction to her, and what it might mean.

She's not your mate, his wiser angels reminded him. *You just haven't taken care of your physical needs lately.*

"Let's check out our dinner," he suggested, indicating the dining table in the open living space.

She headed over, an expectant look on her face.

He enjoyed seeing that she was enthusiastic about eating. Many Maltaffian women seemed to be uninterested in food, or at least pretended to be.

Athena came to stand by his side, her warm weight pressed to his knee.

"That was a long walk," he said. "I'll bet you're thirsty."

"Oh yes," Naomi answered, glancing over.

He looked up at her, confused, then realized she had thought he was talking to her.

Gods, but he was an idiot. What kind of moron talked to his dog like that, especially when there was someone else in the room? And how did he offer Athena a drink first?

Naomi's face went blank for a moment, and then she started laughing.

The sight of the elegant woman doubling over, with her eyes shining and her hair falling across her face, made him laugh, too. Suddenly, the big space was filled with the warm sound of shared merriment.

It felt... nice.

"Sorry about that," he said, after a pause. "I talk to Athena a lot."

"I don't blame you," Naomi said. "She looks like she's listening."

He glanced down at the dog, and she really did look like she was trying to figure out what was going on between them.

"She's a great companion," he said sincerely. "I don't know what I'd do without her."

"Well, it looks like the Center appreciates her, too," Naomi said. "Look at the table."

The pale wood had a single strip of white material along its length, on which were placed half a dozen candles, two glasses of red wine, two plates with steak and vegetables, a basket of breads, and two stainless bowls, one with cut up steak and the other with crystal clear water.

"Wow, Athena," he said. "You'll enjoy this."

He grabbed the bowls and headed to the open kitchen area, placing them on the floor.

"It's heated," he said.

"The floor?" Naomi asked. "I've never seen that before, though I've heard of it."

"Athena's going to love it," he said. "I have to hand it to them. They've really thought of everything."

She gave him a strange smile.

"What?" he asked.

"Nothing," she shrugged. "It's just that a lot of guys in your position seem to never be satisfied."

Gage supposed that was accurate for most security professionals. It was exacting work.

"As I see it," he said thoughtfully. "We're really only here for one thing. And all these extras are just... extra. What is there to complain about when they're making an obvious effort?"

She nodded at him with a thoughtful smile.

"Shall we enjoy some of our *extras*?" she offered.

He fought the urge to blush like a schoolboy at the light flirtation. He was the one who had highlighted the reason for their stay.

"Of course," he said, moving to pull out her chair for her.

"Thank you," she said, sitting.

The scent of her hair made him almost weak-kneed, but he managed to make it back to his own chair and sit.

"To new friends and new adventures," he said, lifting his glass in his best homage to Dayvees Bly-Xarxyn's constant toasts. He felt a little silly, but it seemed like the right thing to do.

"Hear, hear," Naomi said, lifting her own glass, pinky out slightly, as if she had been born to the same society as his employers.

They both took a sip, and she hummed in appreciation.

"You like it?" he asked.

"It's incredible," she said.

"That's a Maltaffian wine," he told her. "So good, they say it's an aphrodisiac."

He sort of wished he could go back in time and hold back that last part. No matter how much he genuinely wanted to take his time and get to know her, his mouth kept steering the conversation back to the bedroom.

But Athena saved him, as usual, choosing that moment to let out a huge sigh as she flopped down on the heated kitchen floor after bolting down her dinner.

"Long day for her," Naomi said.

"She's always on duty, in her eyes," Gage agreed. "I can't seem to convince her that this is like a vacation."

He couldn't really seem to convince himself either, but she didn't need to hear about his obsession with security. She hadn't come all this way to hear him talk about his work.

"You must be exhausted after your journey," she told him sympathetically.

"Not at all," he assured her. "I travel the galaxy as part of my work, and the Fleet-72 I arrived on is equipped with excellent seating and bedchambers. It was nothing."

An odd expression crossed her face and was gone in an instant.

He turned his attention to his dinner, trying to figure it out without looking at her, but he came up with nothing.

The dinner was delicious though.

"So good," Naomi moaned around a bite of steak.

The sound cut through him, making him long to stop all this talking and eating and drag her to bed.

"Wow," she said, looking at the kitchen.

He turned to see Athena was running in her sleep, paws moving. In her sleeping state, the coloration of her fur often shifted to match her dreams. Right now, she was dreaming of a blue sky with fluffy white clouds moving swiftly across it.

"Is that projected onto her somehow?" Naomi asked.

"She's a Drathian Shepherd," he said, shaking his head. "Her fur can change colors based on her thoughts, or to match her environment."

"So, she's dreaming about the sky," Naomi said, eyes locked on the lush blue fur with the drifting patches of white.

"Exactly," he told her.

"Aren't most purebred Drathian Shepherds working dogs?" she asked.

"She is a Maltaffian guard," he told her proudly. "Canine Officer, First Class."

"Wow," Naomi breathed. "So, when you said she thinks she's on duty, you didn't just mean as a pet being a little protective."

"Protecting is her job," he said. "And she is truly accomplished. She once saved two children from a kidnapping attempt."

While he disliked hearing his own *heroism* referred to,

he had no such compunctions when it came to Athena. She had been the real hero that day.

"You are lucky to have her with you," Naomi said with a smile.

"I am," he said. "So, what do you like to do with your free time on your home planet?"

"That's a good question," she said, frowning slightly. "I work for a big law firm, so I don't really have much free time."

So even this Terran had a higher status and better paid job than he did. It was humbling, but he was happy for her if she didn't have to want for anything.

"What kind of law?" he asked, knowing that was the right question, though he probably couldn't ask a single follow-up, assuming he even understood the answer.

"The firm has their finger in a lot of pies," she said. "But the group I'm with handles defense for other big companies being sued for environmental infractions."

He nodded and tried not to wince. Nice as she seemed, Naomi was with the bad guys. It wasn't what he would have expected, given how much she seemed to enjoy the natural world.

"Anyway, it's awful and boring," she said quickly. "On the way to and from, I like to read. When I can get away, it's usually to the mountains. Though that's rare."

"So, you live in a city?" he asked.

"Yes," she told him. "I don't know how much you know about the Terras, but Terra-58 is luckier than most. The capital is beautiful and well-organized. I have an apartment overlooking the park. It's pretty nice."

The Bly-Xarxyns kept an apartment in the city on Maltaffia as well as their regular house, and country homes here and there. Gage knew enough to know that *an apart-*

ment didn't necessarily mean a plain box of a place. It could be a multi-level affair with terraces and a doorman. And if there was a view of a park in a major city, then Naomi must be well-paid for her work indeed. He had heard good things about Terra-58.

"I guess we never would have met if not for this program," he said, shifting uncomfortably in his chair.

Her expression turned sad, and he felt bad for bringing it up.

"Sorry," he said. "I know you have your reasons for being here, just like I have mine."

"On my planet, I'm not eligible to marry, or even date, until I bear a child," she said. "Between that and my work-days, it's just a little lonely, that's all."

"A matriarchal society," he said, remembering. "Of course."

"I'm grateful for this opportunity," she said, putting her fork down and meeting his eyes. "I know this is all a little weird and awkward, but I need you to know how glad I am that you came, and how much I hope this works. For both of us."

Electricity seemed to sizzle between them.

"I am grateful too, Naomi," he told her carefully. "I do not wish to rush you. But would you like to begin our efforts now?"

Her lips parted and she nodded once.

He was up from the table before either of them could say another word.

"Activate privacy mode," he growled, grabbing her hand and marching them off to the bedroom.

7

GAGE

G age willed his heart to stop thundering, and his feet not to move so fast that he frightened her.

But the surge of need that shot through him the moment Naomi's hand was in his felt like someone had flipped a switch inside him.

He needed to touch her, to taste her, to fill her with his seed.

They reached the bedroom and he paused, glancing down at her. The room was spacious, with a bed so big they could practically lose each other in it.

Her dark eyes were fixed on the bed too, as if she craved him as badly as he did her.

Is this the mate bond trying to draw us close?

Choosing not to dwell on the thought, he led her to the bed and kicked off his shoes.

Her eyes locked onto his and she removed her shoes as well.

He loosened his stupid tie and pulled it over his head, tossing it aside with abandon.

She dragged her thumb down the slide of her dress, allowing it to fall open and reveal her lacy underthings.

His own hands froze on the buttons of his shirt as he gazed at the soft beauty of her curves. Everything in him roared and sang for him to claim her.

Her eyes were cast down modestly, as if she were afraid she might not meet with his approval.

He moved to her, taking her hands.

"Naomi," he murmured, his voice deep with wanting. "You are so beautiful."

She squeezed his hands and lifted her chin to meet his eyes.

"If you aren't ready…" he began.

But her hands were moving on his chest, her small fingers delicately releasing the buttons as he tried his best to hold still. When she was finished, he shrugged the shirt off and let it fall to the ground.

She slid her hands down to his belt, but he caught her wrists to stop her.

"Let me concentrate on you first," he whispered, cupping her face in his hand.

Her skin was so soft, like the petal of a flower.

When he leaned down to brush her lips with his, he was so gentle that he barely touched her.

Then her hands were on his shoulders, and she was up on her toes, pressing her lips insistently to his.

He swallowed back a roar of desire and slid his hands to her hips, holding her still even as he longed for her to move against him. He was rigid with lust already, nearly shaking with need and he hadn't even tasted her.

Mate…

The word echoed in his head again, and this time he wasn't so sure it was wrong.

He had never felt this way before. Never. Not even in the arms of the first woman who had taken his pleasure.

Naomi moaned lightly against his mouth, and he thumbed her jaw open, plundering her sweet mouth with his tongue, forgetting the need to treat her like something delicate.

But if she was hurt, she did not show it. Instead, she wrapped her thighs around his waist and pressed her breasts to his chest.

The dual sensations of scratchy lace and warm, soft woman overwhelmed his senses.

He carried her to the bed and placed her down as gently as he could, crawling in to cage her body under his.

"Are you ready to make a baby, Naomi?" he growled.

She nodded, but she was biting her lower lip.

"What's wrong?" he asked, willing himself to slow down.

"I... I've never done this before," she whispered.

"Never?" he echoed, shocked. "But you're a beautiful young woman. You've never wanted to share your bed?"

"Where I come from, women wait until after the arrival of their primary heir before consorting with men," she told him. "And I... I couldn't..."

Gods, forgive him. She couldn't conceive in the clinics. That was why she was here.

Fighting like an animal against his screaming body and longing heart, he pulled back slightly.

This was her first time. It should be special, not a frantic joining.

And whether he wanted to believe it or not, she might just be his true mate. Which meant that claiming her would be for life.

It wouldn't be fair to do that without her knowing and

understanding that this might not be just a surrogacy anymore.

"You don't want me now," she murmured brokenly, misinterpreting his silence in exactly the wrong way.

"I want you desperately," he bit out. "But your first time should be special. Let me enjoy you a little tonight, prepare you for everything to come."

"What do you mean?" she asked him.

"I want to kiss you all over," he told her. "I want to make you feel how good this can be. Can I do that, Naomi?"

She nodded slowly, her dark eyes smoldering.

His own desire was like agony already, but he would not satisfy it tonight. Instead, he bent his head to kiss her again, gently this time, allowing her to take the lead.

When her tongue darted out shyly, he groaned out his approval, his tongue dancing with hers in a mimicry of what he longed to do to her sex.

Her hands tightened on his shoulders, and he pulled back slightly to check on her.

Naomi gazed up at him, her lips swollen from his kisses.

He bent and pressed his lips to her cheeks, her forehead, her eyelids.

She giggled, and the sound flowed over him like a cool stream, refreshing his heated skin.

He kissed a trail from her jawline to her earlobe, and nibbled the tender flesh.

She gasped and arched her back, pressing her lace-encased breasts against his bare chest.

He nibbled and licked his way down her neck, determined to remove the material that separated them.

"I want to take this off," he murmured to her, sliding his hands under her to tease at the slide.

"Yes, please," she whispered, arching her back to make it easier.

A second later, he was peeling the cups away, his mouth practically watering at the sight of her lush breasts, the tips already stiff and needy.

Naomi seemed to be holding her breath.

He bent his head to curl his tongue around one nipple.

The sound she made sent lightning bolts of need down his spine.

Easy, Gage. Easy.

8

NAOMI

Naomi closed her eyes, trying to absorb the exquisite torture of Gage's clever mouth on her breasts.

She had kissed a boy in an alcove at the community school once, felt his heart thrumming against hers as he pressed her awkwardly to the lockers, his hands grasping her hips too hard.

Her own body had responded with a shivering want that went unanswered. Then there were footsteps in the hallway, and it was over.

She should have known, *had known* really, that what happened in that alcove was not the stuff the poets spoke of.

But it was her only basis of understanding. Until now.

Oh, how wrong she had been to even imagine that was a romantic encounter of any kind.

This was what songs were written about, what the holo-films hinted was possible. This was the kiss of pleasure and the ache of need that made worlds go round.

And while a proper Terra-58 woman would not experience it before having a child and husband, she couldn't bring herself to feel guilt.

Not when everything in her was whispering and screaming to her that all she ever needed was more of whatever Gage wanted to give. That she could die happy as long as his hands and mouth were always on her.

"Are you okay?" he murmured, pulling back.

She opened her eyes, ready to cry at the feel of her pebbled nipples in the cold air without his hands and mouth toying with them.

"More," she whispered, shocked at her own wanton demand.

Gage's violet eyes seemed to catch on fire, and he bent to capture her breast in his mouth again.

Something was building in her, tightening and coiling in her center. Her hips were quivering, lifting against him.

He slid a hand down her belly and rested on the scrap of lace that lay between him and her pulsing sex.

Naomi moaned helplessly, her desire pounding, as if that tender flesh had a heartbeat of its own.

"Can I take these off?" he asked her. "I want to touch you."

She lifted her hips, her words lost to her.

He tucked his thumbs under the waistband and removed the last stitch of clothing from her trembling body.

What he did next would hurt, she knew it from the holo-films they showed in health class, explaining what a woman could expect.

And though her breathing went a little shallow at the thought, she wasn't afraid. So long as he touched her, she didn't even care if it hurt.

"Naomi," he murmured. "Are you frightened?"

She shook her head slowly as she gazed into his eyes.

Their violet color had darkened so much that they were nearly black.

"What I do to you tonight will not hurt," he told her. "I only want to make you feel good. Do you want that?"

"Yes, please," she whispered. "Please, Gage."

His eyes went hazy, and she thought for the first time about his need, how he must be holding back.

Her belly tightened again, sending a pleasant twinge through her.

Gage lowered his face to her navel and pressed his lips to her.

A sigh of pleasure escaped her lips, and he growled back at her, pressing kisses to her hips and thighs.

She closed her eyes, overwhelmed with need.

Then she felt something warm and firm slowly stroke the seam of her sex.

"Gage," she gasped, opening her eyes just in time to see him run his tongue along her again.

Wild sensations swept through her, and she nearly cried when he licked her a third time.

"Easy, my love," he murmured to her, as if she were a frightened animal, about to bolt. "I've got you."

He spread her open with a gentle hand and she lost track of her own sounds as he fed on her hungrily, licking, sucking, and tracing circles around her most sensitive place.

The tension in her was peaking, she could feel it in each cell of her body. Every touch of his tongue pulled her tauter until she was crying out and lifting her hips, though whether she was trying to escape the exquisite torture or chase his wicked tongue, she didn't know.

"Gage," she cried out in despair.

Then he was pressing a fingertip just inside to trace a

circle as he latched onto her stiff little pearl and licked while sucking.

For an instant, the world dropped out from under her, as if she were in a crashing hovercraft.

Then pleasure caught her up, slamming rapture through her again and again until at last it allowed her to rest in a warm, delicious peace.

Gage crawled up beside her, pulling her to his chest.

"Wow," she whispered.

He chuckled and nuzzled her hair.

She could smell the scent of her own spice on him, mixed with his own woodsy aroma.

It made her want him all over again. This time the other way, the real way.

"Gage," she murmured, placing her hand on his chest, and then scraping her nails down his pec to the ripple of his hard abs.

He sucked in a breath, and she felt him pulse against her hip.

"No," he said tightly. "That's enough for tonight."

"But—" she began.

"Enough," he said firmly.

She would have argued, but he was running calloused fingertips between her shoulder blades, sending bliss down her spine.

His chest was warm beneath her cheek and the steady pound of his heart was so reassuring she decided to close her eyes for just a moment before seducing him.

9

OBERON

Oberon scanned the day's readings and then rescanned, converting the math and verbiage from their biological input's form into his own system language and back again to ensure accuracy.

No matter how many ways he looked at it, the data always told him the same thing.

Gage wanted Naomi. He was desperate to claim her. Their attraction was off the charts.

But instead of claiming her, he had denied himself the pleasure. In doing so, he had ignored both his own needs and the requirements of the program, as well as making it impossible to impregnate Naomi with his child, his stated goal in being at the Center.

And in spite of his acute unspent arousal, his readings had indicated feelings of satisfaction, and he had slept well.

Oberon tested his logic unit, using a simple test problem and came up in the clear.

His programming was working properly.

As was so often the case when he found himself in a predicament where he didn't understand the actions of his guests, the answer was that the actions of people were not logical.

And since the guests had called up privacy mode, he could not even rely on his biological workmates' opinions. They would never see the footage.

Oberon wasn't used to problems he couldn't solve.

After an illustrious career in his early days, the AI nicknamed Oberon had been acquired for a record-breaking price to design and implement the Midsummer Fertility Center.

At the time, the new mission had hurt his pride, if an AI could be said to have such a thing. He had been trained to plan transport systems and entire cities. But a single highly successful project with a city zoo, where he had created conditions that encouraged endangered species to mate, had sealed his fate.

The Midsummer Center required his services, and they were willing to pay whatever was necessary to secure them, purchasing him outright from his owner company instead of taking a simple project contract, since they wanted him not just to design, but also to implement.

Once his systems were relocated, he was instructed to read every romance novel ever written in order to help him glean an understanding of what biological beings might find romantic.

By the time he had read the hundredth, he had gained a respect and awe for the human emotion called love.

By the hundred thousandth, he knew he did not wish to be a systems architect after all, or at least, not *just* a systems architect.

He longed to be a matchmaker.

However, two things stood in his way. The first was that the couples who came to the Center were matched by an offsite database, which looked at biological compatibility and nothing more. Without the ability to choose a pair, Oberon's chances of making a match were slim.

The second was that even when a likely pair arrived at the Center, Oberon was often confounded by their behavior. He was not, as the novels called living beings, *human*. No matter how attentive a student he was, he could not consistently predict their likes and dislikes.

At times, he couldn't even predict their reflexive reactions, like taking pleasure when it was offered freely and desperately wanted.

However, he had been successful a handful of times so far. Perhaps this effort would prove successful after all, if he was patient and watched the two carefully.

He allowed the data to fall into his back-ups, and focused his efforts on refining the plan he had designed for their day tomorrow to better reflect today's reactions to the Center.

Even if he couldn't understand their behavior, he could control his own designs. And he was determined to offer them a day so romantic, so relaxing and invigorating, that they would be helpless to resist each other.

10

———

NAOMI

Naomi woke to the sound of birds singing and the scent of coffee brewing. Her body was warm and relaxed, and she felt almost like she was still floating in a happy dream.

Opening her eyes, she remembered why she felt so incredible.

Instead of her small bedroom nook back on Terra-58, or her elegant single room at the Center, she was in a beautifully appointed bedroom the size of a museum gallery.

And she was nestled in the warm, muscular arms of a gorgeous, horned alien.

Last night flashed through her head, and she shivered with delight. She hadn't imagined that being touched without a full mating could feel so good.

Gage was very skilled.

That idea had her sitting up and turning to look at his handsome face as he slept. He looked so innocent, lost in his sleep.

He had probably been with so many women though...

The idea kicked up a hot flare of jealousy, though of course she had no claim over the man.

She slid out of bed as quietly as she could, and headed to the bathroom, grabbing her bundle of clothing off the dresser as she went.

Oberon truly thought of everything, and he had deduced quickly that she didn't mind him designing her clothing. By the end of her first few days, he didn't even populate the closet of her room, he simply left a single outfit for her to enjoy.

She showered as quickly as she could, then dressed in the outfit which consisted of a very skimpy bikini that somehow complimented her figure in spite of there not being much material to work with, and a wraparound dress to go on top.

Judging from the choices, she assumed they would be headed to the beach today. Or at least to some sort of water activity.

Slipping her feet into the sandals and tucking the sunglasses into a pocket of the dress, she crept from the bedroom suite out into the living area.

When she emerged from the bedroom, she found Athena standing watchfully in front of the main door. Outside, a small, trim, Terran woman with jet back hair and a lab coat gave her a little wave through the window.

Naomi moved to the door and opened it, not sure how Athena would react.

"Hey there," the woman said in a friendly way. "Hope it's not too early. Oberon let me know you were awake."

"Not at all," Naomi replied, stepping aside to allow the small woman into the house.

Apparently, Naomi's judgement was good enough for

Athena. The dog looked suspiciously at them both for a moment, then paced to the bedroom door and lowered herself back down into a perfect sitting guard position, like a stone gargoyle on a gothic library.

"I'm Dr. Pan," the woman said. "And you must be Naomi. I'm here for your daily check-up."

"Nice to meet you," Naomi said, smiling and feeling a little embarrassed that in spite of the amazing time she'd had last night, there was literally no way she was pregnant today.

"I'll visit with you every morning that you're here," Dr. Pan said. "We do our check-ups even in the early days, when the chance of pregnancy is extremely rare.

"That's fine," Naomi said, hoping her worries hadn't shown on her face.

"How are you feeling today?" Dr. Pan asked.

"Physically?" Naomi asked.

"And mentally," Dr. Pan said. "How are you feeling in general?"

"I feel great," Naomi said honestly. "Is that strange?"

"Not at all, Naomi," the doctor said with an approving smile. "What's the main thing taking up your headspace this morning?"

"I guess just... whether things will work out here," she said, deciding at the last minute not to say what she was actually thinking about.

Gage, Gage, Gage...

"So today you're mainly thinking about the future?" Dr. Pan asked.

"Yes," Naomi replied. "I guess I am."

It felt good to be thinking about the future, even if *the future* was just *tonight*.

She had been so worried about work and her failures at the fertility clinic for so long.

"Wonderful," Dr. Pan said. "Let's get your vitals as soon as you're ready, and then I'll get out of your way."

"Now is good," Naomi said.

The doctor moved around the island and held a sensor to Naomi's forehead.

"Temperature is normal," Dr. Pan said, as her bracelet recorded the results. "Heart rate is normal, blood sugar normal, blood pressure normal."

The hologram above her bracelet shifted and flashed as she went. Her fingers moved gracefully in the air.

"Are you in any pain right now?" Dr. Pan asked, turning back to Naomi, with a serious look in her eyes.

"None," Naomi told her, wondering if pain was common.

Then she thought to what she hadn't done for the first time last night with Gage, and felt her cheeks go hot.

"That's fine," Dr. Pan said. "It's very good."

Naomi smiled at the other woman, feeling suddenly surprised and grateful that Dr. Pan was a Terran of about her age.

Terrans didn't often have high positions intergalactically. And Dr. Pan seemed to be at home in hers.

"Word to the wise," Dr. Pan murmured. "The pastries are unbelievable. Don't miss them."

Naomi glanced over at the island and saw a tray of flaky croissants, glistening doughnuts, and fruit-studded danishes. Her mouth began to water instantly.

"Oh, I'm on it," she said. "I'm ravenous."

"Another good sign," Dr. Pan said, giving her a big smile. "See you tomorrow?"

"See you then," Naomi said as the front door closed behind Dr. Pan.

Naomi grabbed a mug and poured out coffee, then piled a plate with the delicious treats.

The coffee was fresh and hot, and she couldn't help but wonder how Oberon had known when to start it.

She took a bite of a cherry-filled doughnut, and her eyes went back in her head as she moaned in appreciation.

"That good?" a deep voice asked from across the room.

She turned to find Gage, awake and apparently fresh from the shower.

His hair hung damp around his shoulders, and he wore a tight t-shirt and a pair of low-slung jeans. The way he filled it all out made her mouth water even more than the sweet treats.

"Really, really good," she told him with her mouth full, too glad to see him to remember her manners.

"Hm, I'll have to try one too," he said striding over slowly.

"You can have a bite of mine," she offered, holding out the doughnut.

"Are you sure?" he asked. "I take big bites."

"I'm sure," she told him.

He came so close that he was nearly touching her, then bent and ate her doughnut in one bite.

"Whoa," she breathed. "Oh, but there's just a little..."

"A little what?" he asked.

"Just, on the corner of your mouth," she said.

He bent down further.

She went up on her toes in a fit of indulgence and licked the sweet cherry from his mouth.

"Mm," he said. "I can tell why you like these."

Then he was kissing her, tangling his hands in her hair, and pressing her to the counter so that she could feel how much he wanted her.

She was ready to take him, up on the counter, down on the floor, wherever he wanted her.

But he pulled back.

"Naomi," he said gruffly. "There's something we should talk about."

11

GAGE

Gage looked into the beautiful dark eyes of the woman he prayed would be his mate.

Resisting his need to claim her now was nearly impossible.

He wrapped his hands around her upper arms, to keep them off her hips as much as to hold her attention.

Not that he needed help with that. She was gazing up at him like he hung the stars.

"What is it?" she asked, her soft voice sending a shiver of lust down his spine.

"Do you know much about Maltaffians?" he asked her.

She bit her lip and then shook her head.

"Well, there's plenty to learn, but overall, we share more traits with Terrans than not," he told her.

Her eyes went to his horns, and he closed his eyes for a second against the image of her caressing them with her delicate fingers.

Focus.

"But there is one important thing that separates us," he told her. "Do you know what a mate bond is?"

"Like birds have?" she guessed. "They mate for life?"

"Yes," he told her. "Maltaffians have the capacity for a mate bond, though not every Maltaffian is lucky enough to find their true mate."

"But you might," she said, blinking as if she were coming out of a happy dream and into reality. "One day, you might meet your true mate."

"I have already met my true mate, Naomi," he told her gently.

She wiggled out of his hold and put the kitchen island between them, her usual elegant movement now choppy and anxious.

"Does she know you're here?" she demanded. "Is she okay with *this*?"

He stared at her in complete confusion for a moment before he put together what she was saying.

"Naomi, no," he said, shaking his head and trying to organize his thoughts.

"She doesn't know, or she isn't okay with it?" Naomi demanded, her voice high and reedy.

"I explained this all wrong," he said, leaning on the counter and putting his head in his hands. "There is no other woman."

"*Escape me now*," Naomi said.

Instantly, the room around them disappeared. They were no longer standing in a kitchen, but in a blank white space. The food and platter were still there, but they rested on a plain white box rather than the island.

Athena didn't budge, and he wondered for a moment how convincing it had all been to her superior senses.

"How can I help you, Naomi?" Oberon asked.

If he hadn't known Oberon was an AI, Gage would have sworn he sounded fiercely protective.

"We've had a misunderstanding," Gage said. "It's my fault."

"This is beyond a misunderstanding," Naomi said immediately. "He has a true mate, and she doesn't know he's here."

"Gage," Oberon said, before he could respond. "May I have your permission to disclose your relationship status to Naomi?"

"Yes," Gage said. "Please."

"Gage Zeyr'n is single," Oberon said. "Further, he has not had a romantic encounter in at least two years prior to his arrival at the Center."

Gage swallowed his pride. It was kind of mortifying to have his lack of sexual activity announced like that. But Naomi had no prior sexual activity, so she was hardly one to judge.

"I don't understand," Naomi said.

"May I explain better?" Gage asked her. "Privately?"

She nodded.

"Privacy mode confirmed," Oberon said.

Instantly, the space around them repopulated and the house appeared as it had before.

"I'm so sorry," Gage told her. "I guess you know now that I'm a little rusty when it comes to talking to a woman I care about."

"Okay," she said. "So, what's going on?"

"*You* are my mate," he told her simply.

She blinked at him, as if she had forgotten how words worked.

"Can't you feel it?" he asked her. "I know you haven't been with anyone else. But can you feel the pull, the fire between us? That's special."

She nodded slowly, but didn't move closer to him.

"I know you came here to help me," he said. "And so that my seed would awaken your womb. But things have changed now."

He moved to her, coming as close as he dared without touching her.

"If we go through with this project, it won't just be a mating," he explained carefully. "It will be a claiming."

"What does that mean?" she asked.

"It means that I will need to be by your side forever," he told her. "I will protect and comfort you. I will fill your womb, not just with this child, but with as many more as you will allow. It means it will be my whole job to love and cherish you for as long as we live."

She sucked in a breath and her eyes went slightly hazy.

"I will share in your joys and your troubles, forever," he assured her.

Suddenly her eyes widened slightly, and she backed away from him.

"You don't want this?" he asked her, pain slashing through his heart.

"I-I have to think about it," she stammered.

"Is there someone else?" he asked her. "Someone back on your home world who you want to be with?"

She shook her head.

"You don't like me?" he asked.

"Of course I like you," she said. "You're handsome, amazing at... *you know*. And although I'm not sure how many babies I want, I know you would be able to provide for them and then some. I just, I need time."

He longed to demand that she tell him why. He knew she was screaming with pleasure last night. They got along so well already, and the mate bond would ensure that they only took more joy in each other's company.

But he had no right to make that demand.

Had she responded as he hoped, with happiness, he would have told her the other thing she needed to know before accepting.

He'd been so fixated on figuring out why he was so drawn to her last night, that he hadn't stopped to think about the impression he had made on her.

During his morning shower, it hit him that he had arrived here in a fine suit and talked about flying around the galaxy in a high-end craft.

Add to that the fact that a project at the Center cost what it did, and it was easy to see how Naomi would assume he had wealth beyond her imagination.

Would she really be eager to seal a mate bond with a man who lived in a property cut from another man's estate? A man who earned a respectable living and no more, and preferred the idea of digging around in his vegetable garden to glamorous intergalactic travel?

Based on the life and career she had already chosen for herself, he suspected the answer was no.

As his heart shivered in agony, Gage realized the only thing he could do was to keep his mouth shut a little while longer. When she was feeling calmer, he would find a way to tell her. If he said too much now, he risked losing her completely.

She already says she has to think about the mate bond. The money I don't actually have was probably the only thing she liked about me.

"We should turn off privacy mode," Naomi suggested.

"Exit privacy mode," Gage said, still feeling shaken.

"Would you like to hear about today's plans while you eat your breakfast?" Oberon offered, not acknowledging anything he had seen before or after privacy mode.

"Yes, thank you," Naomi told him, perching on a stool without even looking in Gage's direction.

12

NAOMI

Naomi gazed out over the beach at the frothy waves of the ocean rolling in along the golden sand. The world looked like a painting this morning. It was hard to remember why she couldn't just relax and let her joy unfurl.

What woman wouldn't clamor to be claimed by a man like Gage - so gentle, handsome, and skilled at making her feel good?

But Naomi knew better than to let herself believe that the version of him she saw here was the version of him that lived in the real world.

In her experience, men with his kind of money were often spoiled, impudent pigs. And those were usually the nicer ones.

Here at the Center, the world *did* revolve around Gage and his needs. But out there, she figured she would start seeing another side of him the moment he wasn't getting what he felt was his due.

And even if he turned out to be the one red supergiant in a galaxy of stars - a wealthy man without a horrible ego -

there was her own impossible baggage standing in their way.

It was one thing to have risked her own safety and future happiness, but it was another altogether to put Gage's assets at risk because of what she had done.

And how in the world was she supposed to tell him? For all she knew, he would turn her in.

I don't regret what I did, she reminded herself. *I did what was right, and I knew there would be consequences.*

But by all the stars, she had never thought true love might be on the table, however unlikely.

And she'd traded it away before she'd even known it was a possibility.

"What do you like to do at the beach?" Gage asked gently.

"I don't get to the beach very often," she admitted, forcing herself back to the present.

"But you did when you were a child?" he asked.

"Yes," she said, smiling. "My parents used to take us. We built sandcastles."

She thought fondly of those times. Her parents had died in a hovercraft accident a few years back. She made it a point to hold her memories close.

"How do you build a sandcastle?" Gage asked. "Would you like to build one now?"

"Well, we'd need shovels and a couple of pails," she said. "We used to bring a few kitchen tools, too. I mean we can try one without, but it's much easier with those things."

"Will these do?" Oberon's voice asked.

They followed Athena over the next dune to find a stack of buckets, bowls, shovels, and spatulas waiting on the sand in front of them. The dog gave them a cursory sniff, and then moved on after she judged they weren't a threat.

"That's perfect, Oberon," Naomi laughed, feeling excited. "Let's bring these down closer to the water. We'll build an amazing castle."

Gage smiled down at her and grabbed everything in one arm, offering her the other.

She took it shyly, closing her eyes at the feeling of rightness that unleashed in her blood the moment they touched. She hadn't wanted to say anything earlier, but she *did* feel the pull between them. She tried not to let herself think about what it would feel like when he claimed her.

If he claims me, she reminded herself sternly. *But he won't. I can't allow it.*

"Maltaffians prefer to remove their shoes in the sand," Gage said. "It is pleasant to feel sand between the toes."

"Terrans do too," she told him. "Should we?"

"Sure," he said, grinning.

They both kicked off their shoes and she picked up both pairs and carried them in her free hand as they headed toward where the cerulean waves met the golden sand.

It was a beautiful day, just warm enough that she didn't mind the breeze coming off the water, just cool enough that it wasn't unpleasant to crawl around in the sand, finding the ideal place to build a castle.

"Here," she said at last.

"The tide will come in higher," Gage said, frowning.

"That's the magic of a sandcastle," Naomi said smiling. "It's only here for a moment."

"How do we begin?" Gage asked, joining her on the sand.

"First we decide what the castle will look like," she told him. "Let's just build it with buckets and bowls to get an idea."

The morning passed pleasantly as they planned their

castle and moat, shaped the turrets, and decorated with tiny stones and seashells they found along the sand.

Athena lay a few feet off, her back to the water, keeping watch over the beach. Her lush fur had faded to the color of the golden sand so that someone passing by might not even realize they had a guard dog.

Oberon had tried launching flying discs and balls for her to chase, but the formidable beast merely stared at the toys, as if she could set them on fire with her dark eyes, and watched them crash onto the beach.

At last, the final touches were finished on the castle and Naomi leaned back to look.

"It's perfect," she decided. "Now for the moat."

"Should we fill it up?" Gage asked her with a smile.

"Yes," she told him.

"Hang on," he said.

She watched as he leapt up, bent to grab a bucket, and then headed down toward the waves.

The sun glimmered in the slender golden chains that hung from his horns and his muscles flexed as he strode as gracefully as the hunting cats at the City Zoo. He was mesmerizing, and Naomi was left wondering how she could possibly resist him.

He returned with a happy smile on his face. She realized that this was the most relaxed she had ever seen him.

"Ready?" he asked, crouching beside her.

"Be gentle," she cautioned him.

His eyes flashed with fire at her unintended double entendre, but he merely nodded at her.

They both watched as he slowly poured water into the trench around the little castle. It began to soak back into the sand quickly, but for a moment, it looked like a real moat.

"The tide is getting higher," Gage said, glancing

worriedly back at the water. "Maybe we should have built it further away."

"I told you, that's the magic of a sandcastle," she reminded him as she watched the level of the moat drain down almost to nothing. "It doesn't last forever. You have to enjoy it in the moment."

"Like gardening," he said, nodding thoughtfully. "You plant, weed, harvest, and start over again. The joy is in the experience."

"You're a gardener?" she asked him, slightly surprised.

"Yes," he said. "Is that so strange?"

"I don't know," she admitted. "I guess I thought if you traveled so much for your job, that wouldn't be something you could do."

She held back her further opinion that gardening was for patient people who loved a simple life, not for rich galaxy-trotters, like Gage.

"When I return home, I will not be traveling as much as before," he said. "I have a garden that I plan to spend lots of time in."

The baby. Of course.

She smiled up at him, glad that he wasn't planning to drag a child all over the universe.

"Now that your sandcastle is complete, would you like to try body boarding?" Oberon offered.

Gage arched an eyebrow at Naomi.

"Sure," she said, feeling almost giddy with excitement.

"Excellent," Oberon said.

For a moment, the sun seemed to shine a little brighter, as if the fluffy clouds had suddenly parted.

Then things were the same as before, except for the two body boards that appeared beside them on the sand. One was a faded purple, like the bikini Naomi wore under her dress. The other was slightly larger, in a pale green that matched Gage's skin tone.

They got up and peeled off their clothes.

Naomi was a little shy about her skimpy bikini at first. But when she saw Gage wore a pair of form-hugging trunks, she was too distracted to think about herself anymore.

Excitement bubbled in her chest as she raked her eyes over what looked like miles of hard muscle.

When her eyes reached his face, she realized he was staring at her body, too.

Heat flooded her senses, and it took everything she had not to fling herself into his arms.

"Ready?" he asked.

You have no idea...

"Yes," she said.

His eyes were slightly hazy with need as they met hers, but when she bent to grab her board, he followed suit.

Laughing, she jogged down to the water, knowing he would follow.

The warm water tickled her toes as it retreated, leaving tiny, shelled creatures wiggling under the sand.

When it rushed back in, she turned to see Gage was behind her, with Athena by his side, a furrow in her furry brow.

"Athena, did you want to swim too?" she offered, using her regular voice with the dog, as she had heard Gage do.

Athena ignored her completely, and Naomi tried not to let it hurt her feelings. She was a working dog, after all, and it wasn't her job to make friends.

"Do you know how to do this?" Gage asked.

"Pretty much," she said. "We just run into the water and let the waves carry us back on the boards, right?"

"That's the idea," he said. "Let's do it."

They waded into the warm water. Somehow, the glare from the sun wasn't too bright on the surface. Naomi realized that must be Oberon's work.

It was strange to know she was on the beach by the feel, the scent, and the sounds, and at the same time to know that some parts of it were real and others were not.

"This seems like a good place to start," Gage said, when she was in about chest deep.

She turned back to the shore, and they waited for a wave.

Athena patrolled in water up to her shoulders. The fur on her body had morphed into a glorious blue, the color of the water. Her head was the pale color of the froth on the waves.

When the next good wave came, it almost took Naomi by surprise. She jumped at the wrong moment and missed it, getting nothing but a mouthful of salty water for her trouble.

Gage rode his toward the shore, with Athena barking frantically at him all the way.

Then he swam back out, laughing, and joined Naomi again.

This time, when a big wave came, they took it together, and it felt like flying.

But Athena snapping at the waves and board definitely put a damper on the feeling.

"This is scary for her," Naomi said. "And I'm getting tired anyway."

Gage got a strange look on his face, then smiled tenderly at her.

"Your lunch awaits you at the tiki bar," Oberon said, before she could figure out why Gage was looking at her like that.

13

GAGE

Gage held Naomi's hand in his as they approached the little tiki bar he had seen when he first arrived.

Confusion stormed in his chest, and he had to struggle to stay focused on the present and the little woven shack where they would eat lunch and get to know each other even better.

He had never known anyone to be sensitive to Athena's needs before. No one but himself. Most people treated the dog like nothing more than a tool, if they paid her any mind at all.

It was odd to see how much it meant to him that Naomi wanted to stop an activity she was enjoying, not because Athena was annoying her, but because the dog was *scared*.

For all her elegant manners and her corporate job, Naomi clearly had a heart. It was one thing to be considerate to Gage, who she thought was a wealthy suitor. It was another to be concerned for Athena, who could not speak for herself, had no power or wealth to convey, and had done nothing but rebuff Naomi's attempts at friendship since the moment they had met.

It was wonderful to know that his mate had a kind heart. He was so happy that he felt like he could fly. Her beauty was nothing compared to this.

"You're excited for lunch?" she asked, her sweet, teasing voice like music to his senses.

"I guess so," he told her, not wanting to embarrass her by making a big deal out of what she had done. "I'm happy to do anything, if I get to do it with you."

Maybe he could tell her the truth about himself now. Seeing this side of her gave him a confidence he hadn't possessed earlier.

They sat at a small table, set with glasses of bright liquid with fruit on tiny sticks.

"What's this, Oberon?" Naomi asked.

"Cocktails," Oberon told her mysteriously. "Enjoy. Your ceviche will be out in a moment. That requires a biological staff member for preparation."

Naomi smiled at Gage and lifted her elaborate glass of alcohol and fruit.

He lifted his to hers, helpless to resist, and the glasses made a satisfying clink.

The morning on the beach had left him thirsty, and he downed his beverage all at once. It was delicious, cold, and sweet.

Naomi looked up from hers and eyed his glass, looking impressed.

"Oh wow," she said. "I guess I'd better catch up."

He watched in awe as she gulped down her whole drink, then placed it on the table, wiping her mouth on her arm.

"You didn't have to do that," he said.

"We're on vacation, right?" she laughed. "I haven't gotten

away from the office in years. I guess it's time to enjoy myself."

He didn't like the idea of his vibrant mate locked in an office, a servant to the gods of money, for years without ceasing.

Even here on the beach, she built a castle. And she said what made it special was that it was finite.

He tried to crush down his doubtful side, but it was hard to have this sudden reminder of all the reasons why this might not work, whether she was kind to Athena or not.

Athena herself lay by his side, having finished the bowl of water that had awaited her there.

Meanwhile, Naomi was giggling a little, her cheeks pink.

"What's so funny?" he asked.

She pointed to their drinks, which were full again.

"We don't have to drink those," he reminded her. "And we definitely don't have to drink them in a hurry."

"I think I kind of want to," she confessed, still giggling.

Before he could stop her, she had grabbed hers and was lifting it up.

"To new friends," she said. "And an escape from the real world."

He lifted his glass, smiling indulgently at her, and they clinked.

Then he watched as she downed her drink.

"Hey," she said, brow furrowed. "That one wasn't as strong."

"All alcoholic beverages at the Center are mixed perfectly to allow you to enjoy yourselves without regret," Oberon said. "It is one of the advantages of having access to your vitals at all times."

"Seriously?" Naomi said, scowling.

Gage tried to hide his smile.

"Very seriously," Oberon told her. "Your blood alcohol content is currently optimal for relaxation, yet low enough that you will not suffer adverse aftereffects."

"Amazing, Oberon," Gage said, shaking his head in admiration. "Truly amazing."

"Hmph," Naomi sighed. "Thank you for telling me."

"It is my pleasure to explain anything about the Center that you do not understand," Oberon told her.

Her expression was so priceless that Gage couldn't resist laughing out loud.

She reached over and smacked his arm.

He caught her wrist in his hand.

"Why do you want to get drunk anyway?" he asked her.

She shrugged.

He kept hold of her wrist and gave her his most serious bodyguard stare.

"Doesn't it all just seem like... a lot?" she whispered. "The thing you told me this morning, us being here, trying to have a baby?"

"And you think drinking will help?" he asked.

"Well, it can't hurt," she muttered, and then giggled at her own joke.

Stars, but she was adorable.

Even if he didn't like the idea of his tender Terran mate being even more vulnerable than she was the rest of the time, he had to admit she was cute when she was a little tipsy.

"Besides," she confided. "What if I'm too scared to say yes to you when I'm sober?"

A wave of possessive need washed over him at her words, and he tightened his hand around her wrist.

"When you accept my claim, Naomi Peterson, you will

do it stone cold sober," he told her sternly. "And you won't just say yes, you will *beg*."

Her eyes widened and her lips parted slightly.

"Lunch is served," a female voice said from behind the bar.

Gage turned to see that a Maltaffian woman with a chef's hat perched between her horns carrying over a tray with a bowl of fresh ceviche, chips, and dishes.

"How lovely," Naomi said politely, her perfect manners still intact, in spite of the buzz of her fruity beverage. "What is it?"

"Ceviche is a dish made of fresh fish and spices," the chef said. "The fish is marinated in citrus juice to cure it, making traditional cooking unnecessary to achieve a firm and pleasant texture. Most people enjoy eating it with fresh baked chips."

Naomi nodded politely, her expression frozen.

"Bon Appetit," the chef said, backing away.

"Gage, it's not cooked," Naomi whispered to him.

"I think it may as well be cooked," he told her. "Isn't this a Terran thing?"

"Not *all* Terrans enjoy eating raw fish," she hissed. "I don't even eat sushi."

"I'll try it," he offered. "If it's not good, I'll tell you."

She smiled at him like he was her warrior in Invicta armor, and he felt his chest swell with pride, even though he knew what he was doing was a silly little thing.

He scooped up some of the fish and fruit concoction with a chip and brought it to his lips.

The scent was incredible, and it tasted like summertime, the fish so perfectly cured it practically melted on his tongue.

"You like it," Naomi breathed, stunned.

"I really do," he told her. "I think there's mango in there. Do you want to try a small bite?"

"Yes," she said, looking proud of her own bravery. "I'll try some."

He grabbed a chip and fixed her a perfect bite with a chunk of mango and a tiny cube of the tender fish.

She smiled at him as he held it out to her. And instead of taking it from him, she bent to eat it right out of his hand.

Mesmerized, he watched her beautiful face as she swirled the new taste in her mouth.

"Mmm," she hummed. "That *is* good."

"More?" he offered.

She nodded enthusiastically.

He loaded another chip with a perfect bite and fed it to her, loving the way the tip of her tongue brushed his finger.

He continued to feed her for a few dreamy minutes, wishing he could memorize the way her hair slid back as she sat up to chew, the sunlight making her dark tresses shimmer with hints of chestnut.

Then the buzz and beep of her bracelet cut through their happy haze.

She scowled at it, glancing down. Then her eyebrows went straight up.

"I have to take this," she said, scrambling out of her chair and off toward the palm trees. "It's work. I'll be right back."

He watched her dash off, as if the sound of the bracelet had instantly sobered her.

14

OBERON

O beron ran a sequence categorizing and tracking Gage's probable emotions based on his vital signs.

It seemed that each new day presented a new challenge interpreting and reconciling data of one kind from his biological subject's words, another from actions, and a third from physical and emotional responses.

It all wove together in a very complicated web that often didn't make sense, since it was common for one data type to directly contradict the other.

Today, he was learning that Gage's own reactions were woven with those of Athena, and hers with his, so that in order to understand the evolution of Gage's relationship with Naomi, he had to begin with details as seemingly unrelated as what was left in the canine's food dish and whether she napped or sat at attention by Gage's side.

The last few hours had been a tangle of reactions and emotions from all three of them that left Oberon with more questions than answers.

But one thing was clear.

When Naomi expressed concern for Athena, Gage experienced a surge of dopamine in his system that was the equivalent to being offered a delicious meal or a rare sexual experience.

But caring for the dog was Gage's duty, not Naomi's, a series of tasks he continued to fulfill even now as the dog remained by his side.

Was there something Oberon had missed in the normal sequence of biological bonding?

In order to broaden the parameters of his research, he searched and assimilated information not just about the role of canine guards, but about the personal relationships between guards and their canine partners.

He was shocked to find that the emotional sequences experienced by the guards and soldiers made their partners appear more like pets or even children as far as their expressions of appreciation and their continued actions to protect and care for them *after* their years of duty were completed.

Some canines still in their prime retired with their handlers, in spite of expensive and painstaking training. And some handlers adjusted their lifestyles to allow comfort for their canines later in life, even choosing dwellings and travel options based on the canine's needs.

He became so engrossed in this stunning research that he nearly missed it when Naomi's vitals shifted from pleasure to high-stress. Fortunately, a pre-programmed alert roused him from his analysis.

Relinquishing his newly-found understanding of Gage and Athena, he placed his attention on Naomi's pulse and heart rate.

Something was upsetting her quite a bit.

15

NAOMI

Naomi ran as far as she dared without risking that the call would be sent to message holding.

She couldn't risk Gage hearing her, if this call was about what she thought it was. Or anyone else, for that matter.

"Oberon, confirm privacy mode," she hissed.

"Privacy mode confirmed," Oberon said as her bracelet shivered for the fifth and final time.

"Hala?" she gasped, darting behind a palm tree and leaning against it to catch her breath.

"Naomi," Hala whispered. "Are you okay? Where are you?"

"Um, a fertility spa," Naomi remembered to say.

The Midsummer Fertility Center, and the agency who sent her here, made her sign NDAs, agreeing not to disclose that she was here or what she was doing.

They suggested she tell anyone who asked that she had been at a fertility spa, so that if her first clinic treatment after returning home worked, no one would be suspicious.

"Right," Hala said sympathetically. "I hope it works out for you."

As Naomi's desk mate, Hala had been privy to Naomi's many attempts at the fertility clinic back on Terra-58. The woman was practically a saint for listening to Naomi mourn her failures again and again. Hala herself had two teens and a set of overactive triplet toddlers at home, making her own life hard in a different way. But she always sympathized with Naomi.

"Anyway, what's going on?" Naomi asked. "Do they know?"

"Oh, they know," Hala said. "Bud Bulgaro came bursting into the corporate offices screaming that someone alerted the Intergalactic Environmental Bureau that there were lowland wolves on the land he was going to develop. And he said he knew someone at the firm had ratted him out."

"Damn it," Naomi breathed. "The firm will figure it out, and I'll be fired."

"Fired?" Hala echoed. "That's nothing. Bud Bulgaro says when he finds the rat, he's going to *kill them* and everyone they love."

Naomi's blood seemed to freeze in her veins and the edges of her vision darkened.

"Naomi?" Hala said. "Are you there?"

"He couldn't have been serious," Naomi hoped out loud.

"I looked into it, and the Bulgaros are connected," Hala said. "People who cross them have a way of disappearing."

"Lowland wolves are endangered animals," Naomi breathed. "It wouldn't have been right to let him just kill them."

"You think it's better for him to kill you, huh?" Hala asked. "I begged you not to do this."

"I know you did," Naomi said. "And thank you for giving me the heads up today."

"What are you going to do?" Hala asked, her voice soft with concern.

"I'm not really sure," Naomi admitted. "But I'm out of town for another week, so I have some time to think."

"If there's any way I can help—" Hala began.

"No," Naomi told her. "I would never want you involved more than you already are. You probably shouldn't even be calling me, though I'm really grateful you did."

She pushed her hair out of her eyes and looked out over the ocean, wondering what she was supposed to do next.

"Do you have family I can alert for you?" Hala offered.

"No," Naomi said. "Just me."

Thinking about the loss of her parents hit her harder than usual because she had thought of it suddenly, making it hard to breathe.

At least she couldn't endanger them further.

"Well, take care of yourself," Hala told her. "And I'll try to keep you posted if I hear anything."

The call ended and Naomi let her hand drop to her side.

She had been prepared to lose her job, though work was the only thing keeping her going lately. She was a hard worker, and surely, she would find another way to make a living, even if she couldn't work in the industry anymore.

But she hadn't been prepared to be in actual physical danger.

And she certainly hadn't thought about the impact this could have on someone else.

She thought of Gage, and her stomach cramped like she was going to throw up her lunch.

The idea of him being in danger because of her made

her want to weep. She hadn't been willing to risk his fortune if he claimed her and the firm sued.

But losing his *life* because of a woman he had just met?

She paced the sand, wondering what to do.

Unfortunately, there wasn't anything she could do from here, except hide out and hope she had the strength to resist the mate bond.

And Gage was waiting for her now, probably wondering what she was up to.

"Exit privacy mode," she said softly.

"Confirmed," Oberon said. "Are you finished with your lunch? I am asking because I thought you and Gage might each like a little spa time to prepare for this evening's activity."

Oberon was offering her time alone to try and relax.

"Thank you," she said, feeling bone-deep relief. "I would love that."

16

———

GAGE

Gage waited for Naomi, trying to listen, and trying to stop himself from listening, all at once.

On the one hand, he had to respect her privacy. Mate or not, she was her own being.

On the other, it was his job to protect her, and she was obviously distressed about something. He had seen her let her guard down a bit to be silly, but the way she had run from him before picking up her comms was different. She had abandoned her elegance and sprinted like she had to put out a fire.

In Gage's experience, that did not mean anything good.

"I've suggested to Naomi that she might enjoy some private time being pampered in one of our spas, to relax and prepare for this evening's activities," Oberon said. "And you would be welcome to do the same."

"What did she say?" Gage asked.

"She agreed that it was a nice idea," Oberon said.

"Then guess I'm game," Gage said hesitantly.

"Wonderful," Oberon said. "I also had an alternate

option for you, if you prefer. Would you like to hear about it?"

"Yes, please," Gage said. He had never been to a spa, and didn't particularly like the idea of being touched and fussed over by strangers.

"It is the goal of the Center to ensure that all our guests are enjoying themselves," Oberon said. "And I have noted some feelings of restlessness."

"I was only worried about why Naomi ran off," Gage told him quickly. "The Center is perfect, just as it is."

"Thank you," Oberon said. "I am gratified that you are pleased."

The lights around the Tiki bar seemed to glow a little brighter for a moment.

"I was speaking of your companion, Athena," Oberon went on. "She is content with her meals and sleeping options, but it may be that she lacks stimulation here."

That was considerate. But it wasn't like Athena could do what she really wanted to do here.

"I know you tried with the toys on the beach," Gage said carefully, hoping Oberon wasn't hoping to take his partner for a grooming or a ball game. Athena was all about work. "I appreciate you thinking of her, but I don't think she really enjoys playing."

"She is a working dog," Oberon said. "She needs work or training to feel her best."

"Exactly," Gage said, relieved.

"I thought she might enjoy running a training mission with you," Oberon said.

"A training mission?" Gage echoed in disbelief.

"I read the training manual for her licensure," Oberon said. "And I incorporated the scoring database into my own systems. I have created a triathlon for the two of you, testing her skills and your partnership. It may remind you of your multi-cycle recertifications."

"Oberon, that's seriously amazing," Gage said. "I know she'll love it."

"When you are ready, follow the path," Oberon said.

Gage looked up and saw tiny solar lights marking a path away from the tiki bar.

"Athena," he said softly.

The big Shepherd lifted her head instantly, ears pricked up, as if she had never been asleep at all.

"Let's go to work," he said simply.

Athena was on her feet in a single, graceful movement.

He got up and headed for the trail, Athena right by his side. He could feel the happy, eager energy pouring off her.

She missed working. More than he could have imagined.

Maybe as much as he missed it.

Even the sleepy, safe lifestyle of the Bly-Xarxyns had given them both a purpose. Now the days blurred together.

The trees opened up to a small clearing.

"Your first mission is a tracking mission," Oberon said in a more serious than usual tone, if such a thing were possible for an AI. "You have sixty seconds to examine the sample on the rock."

Sure enough, there was a handkerchief sitting on a granite boulder.

"Take a look, Athena," Gage told his partner.

She ran for it, going up on her back paws as her front paws rested carefully on either side of the specimen.

Gage came up to stand beside her. Generally, the tracking specimens were only for the canine, but occasionally there was a clue for the handler as well.

He memorized the green markings on the white cloth. There were two stripes, both deep green like coniferous trees against the snowy white material.

"Begin tracking," Oberon announced.

Athena returned to Gage's side without further ado. Though the AI wasn't using the formal training announcements, she clearly understood that the next portion was coming.

"Go, find it," he told her.

She took off, her body a cloudy blur streaking toward the trees.

Gage followed, knowing his own ability to keep up was part of what he would be assessed on.

It felt good to push his muscles and his endurance. He had been running in the mornings, but it wasn't the same. Nothing was the same as running after bad guys, or running to protect a client.

Even standing guard and just knowing he might have to take action kept a steady stream of adrenaline pumping through him.

Ahead of him, Athena let out a deliriously happy yip to let him know she was onto something.

He pushed harder and found her nosing around an open drain.

"Light," he said, lifting his wrist.

His bracelet projected a circle of light that just penetrated the end of the pipe. It was large in circumference, but not large enough for Gage to crawl into.

Athena yipped again, asking permission. Then twice more.

He glanced up at her.

She was quivering all over, grinning at him with her

tongue hanging from the side of her mouth, so eager for a job to do.

"In," he relented. "*Slowly.*"

He was pretty sure there was nothing in Oberon's training session that would actually harm her.

On the other hand, if a bio staff member had set the tracking specimen and then accidentally dropped their keys down a random working drainpipe, it was highly possible that Athena would be off the intended tracking target and chasing down the bio staff member's scent instead.

It was too late to change his mind.

Athena was already crawling into the pipe, her broad tail tracing happy swirls in the air until it disappeared into the darkness.

He expected her to back out again fairly quickly, with another clue.

Looking around the forest, it was hard to imagine that parts of it were fabricated. Everything seemed so real, down to the loamy scent of damp earth and the texture of the tree trunks.

He crouched and pulled a baby starglove shoot.

It gave a little resistance, then popped out of the ground. It had roots, with soil clinging to them.

So, this part of the scenery was real, or so unnecessarily detailed that it hurt his mind to think about.

He straightened as he realized that too much time had passed.

"Athena," he called into the pipe.

A hollow sound that was very much like her excited bark came back to him, faintly.

A cold finger of panic slid down his spine.

"Athena," he screamed.

The sound came back to him again and he chased it deeper into the trees.

Please let her be okay. Please let her be okay.

The land dropped off slightly and he nearly stumbled over rocks and tree roots as he scrambled down.

But the sound had disappeared.

He stopped in place and turned around to face the hillside behind him.

A loud yap echoed out among the trees suddenly and he saw that Athena was standing in the other end of the open drainpipe, her fur an inky color now, a giant smile on her doggy face.

"Athena," he sighed in relief.

She barked once and then launched herself through the air.

He traced her trajectory and realized what she was trying to do.

A single tree branch ran parallel to the ground about halfway between the height of the hill and the forest floor. It was slender, but sturdy looking.

He just wasn't sure it was sturdy enough to hold the weight of a massive Drathian Shepherd.

And even if it was, would she be able to balance on it?

Holding his breath, he said a silent prayer in his mind.

Athena's front paws hit the branch first, and by the time her back paws found their place, the whole branch was already bouncing under her.

She dropped almost to her belly, bringing her center of gravity down and managed to stay on.

When the branch went still, she jumped again, landing beside him with enough force that he could feel the ground tremble slightly.

"Good work," he told her, feeling breathless.

He tried to soak in the moment of knowing that his partner was safe.

But her nose was already on the ground, twitching.

Then she was leaping through the trees again, her fur shifting from the dark blue-black it had taken on in the darkness inside the pipe to the same brown hue as the forest floor.

"Agility," he said to himself, thinking back to her climb through the pipe and her journey down.

Oberon was incorporating the parts of the test so organically he hadn't even recognized the second phase until it was over.

But if tracking and agility were already in motion, he knew what was coming next.

As if on cue, Athena began to bark excitedly ahead of him.

He pushed himself harder, until the forest seemed to blur beside him.

At last, he emerged in a meadow, where Athena stood vigil in front of a dilapidated wooden shack.

A thin stream of smoke emerged from a metal chimney pipe in the waterlogged roof.

Gage made a rounding-up motion with his hand and Athena trotted around to the back of the shed.

"Come out with your hands up," he announced.

A flick and a hum emitted from the shack, indicating that the occupant had activated a blaster.

"I'll give you to the count of three to set down your weapons and come out with your hands up," Gage called out. "One."

The villain inside the shack let out an ugly chuckle.

"Two," Gage said.

Silence.

"Three," Gage yelled, stepping behind a tree.

The predictable flash of blaster fire told him that their target had come out weapons blazing.

Of course, Gage had baited him into it, so it wasn't unexpected in the least. Although this was a potentially dangerous situation, it was all planned.

"Where are you?" the target yelled out.

The blaster flared again.

Gage peeked out and saw the man had only one weapon. He was tromping through the woods toward him.

"Now," Gage yelled.

The man spun toward his voice as Athena bounded out from behind the shack.

Gage sprinted for him, praying that the element of surprise would save him. Even non-lethal training blasters hurt when you took a direct hit.

The man's face went slack with shock.

But Athena was on his back before he could pull the trigger, and his hands went up slightly, taking Gage out of the immediate line of fire.

Gage wrestled the blaster out of his hands as Athena growled in his ear.

The target fell to his knees.

"On the ground, hands over your head," Gage said in his best bored voice.

He secured the man's hands behind his back, then hauled him up to a seated position.

"Good work," he told Athena. "Relax."

Athena knew this word released her from active duty. She leaped and cavorted around the trees and the target, delighted with herself, and at the feeling of a job well done.

"Incredible," Oberon's voice rang out. "You two are an amazing team."

"Thank you," Gage said, feeling a burst of pride in his chest. "We've been working together a long time."

"You completed the training session with flying colors," Oberon said. "And you took about half the time I thought you would need. You now have time to shower and rest before your date tonight."

"Excellent," Gage said.

"You can either walk back to the house to cool down, or I can send a hover unit," Oberon said.

"We'll walk," Gage told him.

"Very well," Oberon said. "Just follow the path."

A purple butterfly fluttered just in front of them and then led off between the trees. It hovered in the air, as if waiting for Gage.

"Let's go for a walk," he told Athena.

She scampered over to his side in a puppyish way, and he couldn't resist smiling at her.

He loved seeing her like this. It had been too long.

"Should we organize some training sessions when we get back home?" he asked her. "That could be fun, right?"

She was practically dancing on her feet by his side.

"It's important for us to be happy," he told her. "Even if our life will be different."

No matter the color of her fur, Athena's eyes were always the same. She glanced up at him now, empathy in the familiar, dark brown orbs.

"It's harder for you than it is for me," he reminded her. "At least I understand what's going on."

Her ears pricked up so much he wondered if she felt the stretch.

"Though if Naomi says yes, things will change more than I can understand, too," he admitted. "I never thought I would have a mate or child. The idea of both is..."

He trailed off, wondering how to describe the feeling.

"I feel extraordinarily lucky and terrified at the same time," he told Athena.

How was his mate going to react when she found out who he really was and how little he had? After all, she thought she was falling for a billionaire, not a bodyguard.

Athena made a chuffing sound, as if she thought both what he was saying and what he was thinking were nonsense.

"You're easy to talk to. You know that?" he told her fondly. "I wish you could understand me and give me some advice. I know it would be spot on."

They walked on for a while, Gage soaking in the peace of the woods, the good feeling of an honest sweat cooling his skin, and the company of his best friend.

When the house finally appeared in the distance, his mind was more in order than before.

"I won't claim her until she knows," he told Athena. "And we'll get to know each other better first."

Athena didn't respond, just trotted along at his side.

For some reason, he was reminded of their first meeting. She had been a fifteen-week-old puppy, already big enough to be awkward, her massive paws nearly tripping her up, telling him she would be gigantic one day.

Her fur was still deciding on a primary color. It had shifted so many times in her excitement when he greeted her that it practically strobed.

But when they walked together, she fell into his rhythm right away, even if she stepped on his foot a couple of times.

He had known from that very first day that this would be one of the most important relationships of his life.

What did it say about him, that he could commit more easily to a dog than to a mate?

He pictured Naomi, her serious eyes fixed on him as she trusted him to bring her beautiful body to life with pleasure for the very first time, so soon after they met.

"Do I even deserve her?" he wondered out loud to himself.

17

NAOMI

Naomi closed her eyes and soaked in the warmth. The scent from the water in the copper tub lifted with the steam, practically hypnotizing her with pleasure.

Soft music played somewhere, low strings with a shiver of soft bells.

Her whole body was already loosened up and euphoric from the massage drone's work and the sweet tea she had sipped before the droids helped her strip and lower herself into the tub.

By the time they were finished, she felt as if she were half asleep and half awake, floating through calm waters.

But the moment the droids closed the doors behind them, leaving her alone in the fragrant warmth, her mind began to spin again.

What am I going to do?

"Oberon," she said. "Are you there?"

"Always," he told her.

"I would like to make a call," she said.

"Calls are not permitted from the Center," he said.

"But I got a call earlier," she protested.

"Your colleague explained that the situation was life and death," Oberon explained. "I was able to grant an exception to let the call through without video feed."

So that was why the call hadn't been via holo.

"I just... feel like I need to talk to a friend," Naomi said. "What if it's someone who is already part of the program?"

"Give me a name," Oberon said. "I can't confirm or deny a participant's status, but I might be able to project a call for you if the one you name is with the Center and wishes to speak with you."

"Thank you," Naomi said, practically tearing up with relief.

She thought of Piper, Haven, and Alexis, but all three were most likely beyond the point of still being at the Center.

"Chloe?" she asked, hoping that Chloe had actually made it.

"One moment," Oberon said.

The soft music seemed quieter and the room larger as she waited. She had never felt more alone.

One of the mirrors on the wall flickered into a screen.

"Naomi?" Chloe said softly.

"Chloe," Naomi sighed happily. "Sorry, I'm in the tub."

"I can't see anything but bubbles and flower petals," Chloe laughed. "Are you getting pampered?"

"Yes," Naomi said. "How about you?"

"Well, sure, but not like that," Chloe said with her signature bright smile. "Hey, I didn't know we could make calls."

"Only to each other, I think," Naomi said. "Privacy mode, please."

"Privacy mode confirmed," Oberon said.

"Oberon mentioned you could use an ear," Chloe said

sympathetically. "What's going on? How's your intended parent?"

"It's not him," Naomi said quickly.

"It isn't?" Chloe asked, her brow furrowing.

"Well, I mean it has to do with him, but it's not him," Naomi said. "He's great."

"He is?" Chloe asked, waggling her eyebrows slightly.

Naomi couldn't help laughing.

Chloe always lightened her heart. It was what made her an excellent teacher too.

"He is," Naomi said. "He's been nothing but nice to me... more than nice. I obviously have to assume he's just another billionaire bastard when he's not here getting spoiled, though."

"Why do you have to assume that?" Chloe asked.

"Because I've worked with, and for, too many wealthy men," Naomi sighed. "They're entitled little pricks the minute things don't go their way. Believe me."

"Hm," Chloe said, frowning. "I guess I could see that."

"But I really like him anyway," Naomi said. "And he's interested in pursuing a relationship, even after our time here."

She didn't dare tell her friend about the mate bond. It was too much.

"And how do you feel about that?" Chloe asked. "Are you going to give him a chance?"

Naomi bit her lip.

"I'm not sure," she said. "But it's not really because of him. It's because of work."

"Work?" Chloe echoed.

Naomi decided it was better to just get it all out.

"I sent an anonymous tip to the Intergalactic Environmental Bureau that the firm's client was going to build on a site that was a habitat for endangered lowland wolves," she said, before she could change her mind.

"Oh," Chloe said, looking stunned.

"I knew the firm would figure it out, and I'd lose my job," Naomi said wearily. "But it was the right thing to do."

"I'm proud of you," Chloe said. "I know you drown your sorrows in your work. What you did was very brave. And I'm sure you'll find another job."

"That was how I was looking at it," Naomi admitted. "I knew it would be awful, but I was pretty sure I could find work in the industry if they didn't blackball me, and in another field if they did."

"Exactly," Chloe said, nodding.

"I didn't think about the client though," Naomi told her. "It turns out that the Bulgaro family was developing the land. And one of them came into the firm screaming that they were going to kill the person who did this, and everyone they love."

"Oh, Naomi," Chloe breathed.

"Now I'm afraid to go home," Naomi told her. "And I'm also afraid to conceive a child with Gage. What if the Bulgaros come after him and the baby?"

"And if you get together with him..." Chloe realized out loud.

"I'd be putting him in even more danger," Naomi said. "I know the Center could come after me for breaking my contract if I don't try, but I don't think I can do this."

"You'll do the right thing," Chloe said. "Even if it's hard, even if there are consequences."

"Yes," Naomi said, feeling relieved. "I can live with the consequences of breaking a contract. I can't live with the idea of endangering someone I care about."

"What are you going to tell Gage?" Chloe asked.

Naomi looked down at the shimmering bubbles in the tub, wishing they could give her an answer.

"I can't tell him what I did," she said softly after a moment. "He's a wealthy man, just like those developers. For all I know, he would turn me in."

"You just said you cared about him," Chloe said, frowning. "I don't think you would care about someone that heartless. Is his money really the only thing you have against him?"

Naomi bit her lip, feeling foolish.

"If that's all, then I think you should trust the instinct that made you like him," Chloe went on. "Talk to him, even if you don't share specifics. You have very good gut instincts, Naomi. I think you might be pleasantly surprised."

"And if not, then at least I know where I stand," Naomi said thoughtfully.

"You'll find the right time to talk to him," Chloe said. "And hey, a guy with money might be able to keep you safe from the Bulgaros."

"He does have an amazing guard dog," Naomi allowed.

"There you go," Chloe said brightly.

"Thank you," Naomi said, meeting her friend's eyes on the screen. "I'm really glad you're here."

"Me too," Chloe said. "Maybe when I meet my match, I'll be calling you back."

"Maybe so," Naomi told her.

An alert popped up on the screen.

～

FIFTEEN MINUTES TO *leave for dinner and dancing.*

～

"Oh shoot," Naomi said. "I have to run."

"You'll talk to him, right?" Chloe said sternly, fixing Naomi with a very serious expression,

"Yes, teacher," Naomi joked, winking at her friend.

Chloe rolled her eyes and then blew her a kiss.

Naomi blew one back and the screen went dark, leaving her alone once more.

"Exit privacy mode," she said.

"Thank you," Oberon voice said immediately. "Did you enjoy your call?"

"I did," Naomi said. "It gave me a lot to think about."

18

GAGE

Gage paced nervously outside the spa, wondering how Naomi was feeling after some time to relax.

If a call had made it through the Center's bracelet filtration protocol, it must have been an important one. And whatever it was about, it had clearly upset her.

Athena was pacing at his side, but part of her attention was taken up by the pair of midnight stallions pulling the floating carriage that was waiting to take them to dinner.

While they had been exposed to all kinds of animals in their training and fieldwork, actual horses were not common on Maltaffia or any of its allies.

And Gage wasn't even sure if these were real horses.

"It's okay, Athena," he told his partner reassuringly. "If they're here, it's because Oberon knows they're safe."

And now I sound as soft as any rich idiot on vacation.

It was probably for the best that Athena wasn't letting her guard down. One of them had to keep their wits about them, and it certainly wasn't Gage.

He was too busy fretting about what Naomi would say when she found out how many credits were in his savings.

The thing of it was, until this week, he would have felt he was doing well. For a man in his position, he had been careful, saved as much as he could, and invested wisely. Even without saving the Bly-Xarxyn kids, he would have retired comfortably one day.

But compared to the jerks at her law firm, he was a peasant. Ten lifetimes wouldn't be enough to turn his savings into assets like theirs, even with a good mind for investing.

The doors to the spa slid open, and the sight of Naomi nearly knocked the wind out of him.

Her dark hair was pinned up, with a few soft tendrils escaping, revealing the elegant curve of her exposed neck. Her dress shimmered, the iridescent silky fabric plunging low to reveal the tops of her breasts, and clinging to her waist before flaring out at the hips and falling nearly to her ankles in gauzy layers.

She looked like a young goddess, ready for a moonlight hunt, or to be wed at midnight under the stars.

His pulse pounded in his ears.

"Hi," she said softly.

"Hi," he echoed, having forgotten every other word.

"Oh," she said, her eyes lighting up as she looked over his shoulder. "Horses."

"Oberon thought you might enjoy riding in a horse-drawn carriage," Gage told her, recovering slightly. "Is that considered romantic on Terra-58?"

"Very romantic," she assured him as she moved gracefully to the horses, extending her hands for them to sniff.

One tossed his mane and clomped the ground with a restive hoof.

But the other nuzzled her palm as if looking for a treat.

"There are carrots on the seat of the carriage," Oberon

said, his voice coming from everywhere and nowhere at once.

Gage jogged over to grab them and bring one to Naomi.

"Thanks," she said, her eyes sparkling.

The friendlier stallion took the carrot, crunching happily while she scratched behind his ear.

While she watched, the other one nudged her bottom.

"Oh," she said in surprise.

Gage tried not to laugh as he grabbed another carrot for her.

"I suppose you want one too," she suggested, holding it on an open palm.

The stallion took it gingerly from her hand and crunched it up without looking at her.

"Stars, but they're gorgeous," she said, stepping back. "I've seen them in the park pulling carriages, but never up close."

"Why not?" Gage asked.

"You know, I'm not really sure," she told him. "From now on, if there's something I'm interested in I'm going to grab onto it with both hands."

He smiled at her enthusiasm.

They headed for the doors of the carriage. Though the seating was up fairly high from the ground, there was no step.

Gage realized it must be Oberon's work. Nothing here had been forgotten. This was an excuse for them to touch.

"Can I help you up?" he offered, extending his hand.

"Thank you," she said, taking it.

He swung her up easily, then climbed in after her.

Of course, the seat was not really wide enough for the both of them. She giggled and got up, allowing him to sit before snuggling herself back in beside him.

As soon as they were settled, the horses began to move, as if they knew the way. And Gage wondered again just how real they were.

Beside them, Athena trotted alongside the carriage, looking the happiest Gage had seen her in a while, other than during the training session.

"Did you enjoy your time at the spa?" he asked Naomi.

"It was nice," she told him. "But this is way more fun."

For a moment, he let himself relax. This was what he was supposed to be doing now, getting to know her, with both of them enjoying themselves.

A short while later, the horses stopped in front of what looked like an old-fashioned Terran house. It was a massive structure with a slate roof, ornate woodwork, and banks of tall windows. Additions jaunted off the main house at odd angles, like an illustration out of a children's book.

Lampposts led down the drive to the sweeping front porch. The horses followed it, their harnesses jingling merrily in time with their hoofbeats.

Gage jumped down from the carriage when it stopped in front of the house, then walked over to Naomi's side and held out his arms.

His heart thundered as she took his hands and jumped, allowing him to catch her and hold her close before lowering her slowly to the ground, her dress sliding against him seductively.

She was standing so close, her sweet scent overwhelming his senses.

He gazed down at her, trying to memorize her dark eyes and lush, pink lips.

The sound of the doors opening pulled him out of her spell and he glanced up to see a butler droid standing in the threshold.

"Welcome," the droid said, with an annoying fancy accent that had obviously been programmed. "Your dinner awaits."

Naomi's hand slid into the crook of Gage's arm as naturally as if it had always been there and they climbed the steps of the ancient-looking building together, with Athena taking her usual position at his heel.

The inside was lit with old fashioned lamps and chandeliers. The scent of something delicious floated down the massive entry hall, making his stomach grumble.

"The dining room is just this way," the droid said, rolling forward on his old-style rubber slide treads.

"They really went the extra mile to make it authentic," Gage said, impressed.

"To be honest, they mixed the time periods a little," Naomi said with a wink. "But I only know because I minored in ancient design. A home from this era was not automated in any way."

"Then it wouldn't have been worth living in," Gage decided.

Naomi laughed, her head tilted back exposing her neck, which he instantly wanted to nibble and kiss.

They followed the droid into a massive dining room with dark-stained wood on the walls and a thick carpet on the floor. The walls were hung with beautiful landscapes all seeming to show the same mountain with a castle on it during different seasons.

A massive chandelier cast light over a sumptuous feast. Bowls and trays of bright vegetables competed for space with platters of glistening meats, baskets of fragrant bread, and bottles of wine. There was even an area near the wall for Athena, with a tray of treats and a soft-looking bed.

"Amazing," Naomi breathed.

"Please enjoy," the butler droid announced, his fake accent decidedly less annoying to Gage now that he had seen this spread. "Ring the bell if you need anything at all."

"Thank you," Naomi said.

Gage moved to her and pulled out her chair, inhaling her sweet scent once again. He nodded to Athena, who took her cue and wandered over to inspect her setup.

When he was seated, a helper drone darted out to fill their glasses.

"Sweet, mulled wine," it announced quietly before darting out of the way again.

"My favorite," Naomi murmured. "To new friends, and new adventures."

He lifted his glass to hers, smiling at her for using his toast from last night.

Soft music began to play through unseen speakers, and Gage piled delicacies onto his plate, trying to distract himself from wondering how he could possibly get through this night without claiming his mate.

19

——————

NAOMI

After the meal, Naomi clung to Gage's shoulders, laughing as he spun her around the ballroom.

Between the dress, the beautiful setting, and the gorgeous man who held her, she felt like a princess in one of the holo-films she had watched over and over again as a child.

Is this what it would be like to be his mate?

Oddly, he seemed as impressed by the evening as she was. But that made no sense. If he could afford the Center, he could afford evenings like this one as often as he liked.

Maybe he was one of those eccentric types, who preferred to hoard his wealth without spending it.

The music swelled and Gage spun her out and then pulled her back into his warm arms, dipping her close to the floor.

She blinked up at him, wondering if he would kiss her now.

You can't kiss him. You can't do anything until you tell him the truth.

She closed her eyes, and he pulled her back up with a flourish as the song ended.

"I think it might be time to get some rest," he said, his voice dark.

His eyes were on the massive windows and the starlight bathing the lawn outside.

Though of course it could have been any time of day. Oberon could make the sky look however he wanted.

Was he angry with her for resisting his kiss?

Or was he desperate to bring her home? So aroused he couldn't even look at her.

The idea made her belly coil with tension.

"The carriage is waiting," Oberon said softly.

Gage turned from the window and strode toward her, offering her his arm again.

She took it and they took their leave of the ballroom, descending the handsome curved staircase to arrive again in the great entry hall where they had come in.

"Thank you for your visit," the butler droid said.

"Thank you," Naomi replied.

Gage nodded his head.

Outside, the horses tossed their heads, inky manes swirling in the air.

Athena trotted up from her resting place, looking content.

Naomi wondered what the dog thought about their evening. The beautiful animal seemed to trust her surroundings more than when she first arrived.

But she was no more inclined to acknowledge Naomi's existence than before. Instead, she trotted right past her and around the back of the carriage to get to Gage's side.

"May I?" Gage asked, holding out his hands.

She took them, and again, he swung her up into the

carriage, seemingly without effort.

"Wow," she said to herself as she waited for him to climb in.

"What?" he asked.

"You're very strong," she said stiffly.

"Thank you," he replied with a lazy grin that made her cheeks tingle. "Ready to go home?"

She nodded as the horses began moving. Athena trotted beside them once more, seeming to enjoy the exercise.

"I hope you'll enjoy tonight's stay," Oberon said. "It's a little different from your first place."

"Tell us about it," Gage said.

"No," Naomi said quickly. "Let's have it be a surprise."

He smiled down at her.

"She's right," he told Oberon.

"Very well," the AI said. "You won't have very long to wait."

The carriage continued. Despite the fact that it was floating above the ground, it still bumped along the dirt path through the trees, jostling Naomi further and further into Gage's warmth - another deliberate design choice, no doubt.

When they went over a particularly large bump, she cried out and had to brace herself not to fall off the bench.

"For the sake of the Rings," Gage growled, putting his arms out. "Come here."

She crawled gratefully into his lap, nearly shivering with pleasure when he locked his big arms around her waist.

It was almost embarrassing how quickly her body responded to his. It took all she had not to wiggle and squirm.

And she could feel how much he wanted her, the thick column of his eager flesh throbbed against her back, and he hissed in a breath every time the jostling of the carriage made her move against him.

How could she possibly make it through another night without allowing him to stake his claim?

Another rough bump wound her up with his face nuzzled in her neck. The sizzle of his hot breath against her tender flesh made her moan lightly.

His arms clenched around her, tight as iron.

Forget making it through the night - it was starting to feel like they wouldn't even make it out of the carriage.

Suddenly, the trees opened up to reveal a lush valley, kissed by moonlight.

A familiar looking castle was nestled within a garden, a moat gleaming in the starlight around it.

"It's the castle from the paintings at the mansion," Naomi realized out loud.

"It looks a lot like the sandcastle we built," Gage added.

"You're right," she breathed.

"Tonight, you'll be staying in this castle," Oberon told them. "And tomorrow you'll participate in activities here, like learning to use an Old Terran bow and arrow, and how to spar with swords."

"Awesome," Gage said, sounding way more enthusiastic than Naomi was about it. She'd never really been one for fighting.

But she smiled indulgently, glad that he would enjoy himself. She was pretty sure ballroom dancing had been more her thing, but he'd ended up having fun tonight. Surely, she could do the same tomorrow. And it didn't sound too bad. Archery had always been her favorite at summer camp.

If we're still speaking, after I tell him what I've done.

Or after I chicken out and avoid letting him claim me.

One way or the other, their relationship was about to sour, and it was all her fault.

The carriage passed over the drawbridge, and she gazed down at the dark water in the moat. She swore she saw movement in there, and then realized it was probably just the reflection of the carriage, warped by the rippling water.

When they arrived in the courtyard, there was a loud creak as the bridge began to slowly lower itself.

Gage helped her down once more and they headed to the entry, Athena trotting along by Gage's side.

The massive carved doors to the castle swung open to reveal a hall with lavish rugs and paintings as well as a row of life-sized, wooden soldiers wearing shining metal armor.

"Tea and cakes are awaiting you in the royal suite upstairs," Oberon said. "You can explore the house now, or wait until morning."

"I'm so tired," Naomi lied, wondering if Gage would really believe she could just fall asleep when there was so much between them.

"Why don't you go up and get comfortable," Gage said. "I'm just going to check out the house a little."

Stunned, she nodded and headed for the stairs.

She hadn't expected him to let her out of his sight. Even she could feel the mate bond pulling taut and painful between them, and they were still practically in the same room.

Don't question it. Just go.

She jogged up the stairs, willing herself to get further away, and hoping that might help.

The landing of the castle's tower was large enough to have more rugs and floating sofas. She found the royal suite fairly easily because of its sheer size. Three of the seven doors coming off the landing led into its various rooms.

There was a library, a sitting room, and then the bedroom itself, with an attached bath.

Hurriedly, she grabbed a lacy nightgown that was laid out on the bed and took it into the bathroom.

Thankfully, there was a modern refresher as well as a porcelain soaking tub with feet. She didn't want to take the time to fill a bath. If she could just get cleaned up and into bed, pretending to be asleep, before Gage came back, she might be in the clear.

Something about it reminded her of being a small child and trying to stay up on Hearth Day Eve without her parents knowing.

Focus, Naomi.

A few minutes later, she was showered and dressed in the flimsy gown. She opened the bathroom door a crack, but Gage wasn't back yet.

As quickly as she could, she dashed across the room and into bed.

Pulling the covers up over her head, she suddenly wondered why he was taking so long downstairs.

It almost seemed like he was avoiding her, too.

But when she thought back to the evening they had shared, and the way he had held her in the carriage, she knew that couldn't be the case.

She tried to doze off quickly, knowing it would be better if she were actually asleep when he came in than if she were faking it.

But somehow, she felt restless, as if there were a compressed spring in her chest.

She listened to the tick of the old-fashioned clock on the wall as she waited what felt like an eternity for sleep to take her.

20

———

NAOMI

Naomi awoke to the sound of a knock on the door. She opened her eyes and for a moment she was truly lost. Nothing was familiar, she didn't even feel like herself.

She had been dreaming that someone was lost, and she was searching...

The knock repeated and she felt the bed creak.

Gage.

He must have joined her at some point, but she didn't remember him coming into the room, and he obviously hadn't tried to wake her.

"Hey," he said, opening the door for Dr. Pan.

The Terran doctor bustled in, a worried look on her face.

"Sorry to disturb you," she said.

"No worries," Naomi replied, forcing herself to sit up and face the day. "I'm sorry I slept so late. I guess you want to get my vitals?"

"We should definitely do that today," Dr. Pan said. "But I got a comm to bring you in to have your security protocols updated on your bracelets when I was on the way here."

"Why?" Gage demanded.

His body language had solidified from relaxed and fluid to tense and ready. Athena, sensing his concern, was suddenly moving to his side, her beautiful ears pricked up.

"I'm not sure," Dr. Pan admitted. "But Oberon can explain more when we get there."

What Naomi took from the doctor's reassuring words was chilling. Oberon *can't* explain now.

She could not begin to fathom the potential bandwidth of the AI who had created and ran this place. Who knew how many simulations he was running at once, and how many potential clients he was planning for at the same time?

If his load was too great to add a single conversation, something was very wrong.

"We should get moving," the doctor said.

Gage was already pulling jeans and a t-shirt over the boxers he had apparently slept in.

Naomi grabbed her clothing and dashed into the bathroom to ready herself.

As soon as she was out, they all moved for the hallway, taking the stairs quickly and jogging through the entryway to hop in the carriage that was parked outside.

Gage offered Dr. Pan a hand, and she practically dove in.

Naomi took Gage's hand and let him swing her up too, waiting for him to board and then sitting directly on his lap, like the night before.

Even the horses seemed to be in a hurry. Their hooves danced and they tossed their inky manes as they waited for the drawbridge to lower.

Then they were off, clattering across the wooden bridge and flying for the path through the woods.

No one spoke.

After what felt like a lifetime, they arrived in a space that looked almost like a town square, with two large, modern-looking buildings. A small park nestled between them, its center was paved and equipped with a fountain and benches.

A line of people in lab coats stretched from one building around the corner of the next.

"Let's go," Dr. Pan said, leaping out of the carriage.

Naomi and Gage followed her as she marched to the front of the line.

"Clients," Dr. Pan announced as they passed the parade of employees. "Clients coming through."

Most of the employees nodded to them or ignored them. Naomi figured they must be used to giving clients priority service here.

But one man tapping his foot near the front of the line got a look on his face like he had smelled something awful when he saw them going first. He was carrying what looked like a heavy backpack and sweating a little under his load, so Naomi could hardly blame him for being frustrated.

She mouthed the word *sorry* as they passed, but he looked away.

When they reached the main doors, a large, Bergalian security guard stepped in front, blocking their path.

"Authorized personnel only," the big, furry man said flatly.

"We are authorized," Dr. Pan retorted, holding up her bracelet.

"Not all of you," he responded, eying Athena suspiciously.

"Of all the..." Dr. Pan began.

"It's okay," Gage told her. "We don't need to make a fuss.

It will be better if we just get in and out. Athena can wait for us out here."

Athena moved beside the guard and sat, her tongue lolling slightly out of her mouth as she panted from the run.

"We'll be right back," Gage told her as they stepped inside.

"This way," Dr. Pan said, opening a door and ushering them inside.

A massive foyer welcomed them. Big windows revealed the parklike setting outside, and a holo-screen on the far wall streamed news from all over the sector.

Dr. Pan led them past more employees, toward a corridor.

21

GAGE

Gage had a distinctly bad feeling as the young Vystian staff member slid his thumb over Naomi's bracelet.

It wasn't just that the Vystian was extremely good-looking, with shivering tentacles flowing from his head like hair, or that he was gazing unapologetically at Naomi's breasts, with an expression of frank appreciation on his handsome face. That was just surface jealousy.

But Gage's gut was rumbling, telling him things weren't right. And he'd learned long ago to trust his instincts.

He cursed himself for not insisting that he be allowed to bring Athena inside.

He missed her attentive eyes and clever snout.

And her vicious sharp teeth.

"There," the Vystian said, smiling dangerously at Naomi. "You're all set now."

"Thank you," she said, apparently not even noticing his open flirtation.

Gage stepped in before the boy had a chance to wave

him forward. He didn't want to be taking orders from the little creep.

"What's actually going on here?" he demanded, thrusting his arm forward so the kid could adjust the bracelet.

"Just standard procedures," the boy drawled importantly. "A precautionary measure."

"A standard precautionary measure because of what?" Gage asked.

"Excuse me?" the kid said, sliding his thumb over Gage's bracelet.

"A place like this doesn't drag clients out of bed and stand highly trained employees in line for nothing," Gage said quietly, but articulating his words so the kid would know he was serious.

The boy opened his mouth and closed it again.

"Apologies," Oberon said.

Though his voice was the right timbre and seemed to float in the air at the usual distance above Gage's head, it seemed thin, almost *flat*.

"Oberon," Naomi said happily.

"There has been what some might consider a sophisticated attempt to hack into the Center's system," Oberon said in his flat voice. "Fortunately, given my security, it was rudimentary and easy to shut down. But out of an abundance of caution, we are updating all security codes, and I am analyzing and running every segment in the Center, many of them at once. This is why my voice may not have its full dynamic range, and why I sent Dr. Pan to speak with you earlier. However, you may rest assured that as long as I'm online, the Center is completely safe."

"Understood," Gage said. "I'll let you get back to it."

"Thank you, sir," Oberon said.

Gage set his jaw and let the kid keep swiping and tapping his bracelet.

"It really is normal to change the codes," Naomi said quietly to Gage. "They reprogram our bracelets at work all the time."

Gage nodded, afraid that if he spoke, he might not be able to stop.

The young man finished his work in silence.

"You're good," he said at last.

"Thanks," Gage said brusquely.

Naomi gave the boy a little wave, then grabbed Gage's arm and they headed out.

Gage clenched his jaw and tried to hide the depth of his concern. Who would try to hack a fertility clinic, and why?

He pulled her into a little nook in the foyer of the building and swiped at his comms, trying to see if there was any lag.

Employees moved through the open space, in line to have their bracelets updated by the small army of security personnel at desks just like the Vystian's.

"You okay?" she asked him.

"Something's not right," he said, scanning the lobby, trying to figure out what had his senses tingling.

Great Rings, but he missed Athena.

As if in response to his thought, there was a commotion by the doors to the foyer. Something was moving quickly through the space, causing people to react with surprise.

A familiar cloudy gray body bounded toward Gage, tail swinging back and forth with excitement.

"She missed you," Naomi said.

But Gage knew better. Athena would never leave her post without a reason. Something had brought her inside.

Athena turned to Naomi, acknowledging her existence

for the first time since growling at her in the café, what felt like a hundred years ago.

"It's very nice to see you, Athena," Naomi said politely.

Athena studied her for a moment, as if considering, then erupted in a cacophony of barking.

"Oh, no," Naomi sighed.

"You aren't what she's barking at," Gage said, scanning the foyer once again.

Athena took off toward the doors and Gage followed with his eyes.

"Wait," he said, his eye catching on a familiar figure. "Wait, wait, wait…"

"What's going on?" Naomi demanded.

But Gage was already moving, imploring his muscles to launch him faster and faster.

The man who had been sweating and tapping his foot at the front of the line earlier was just inside the doors now.

And he wasn't wearing the backpack.

"Bomb," Gage yelled. "Get out. Bomb!"

The lobby filled with the sounds of panic as the people inside all ran for the doors, creating a hopeless tangle of bodies.

A tug at his heart told him Naomi was nearby. But there was no time to chase her away.

He reached the place where he had seen the man, and sure enough, the backpack sat on the ground, emitting a beeping sound he hadn't been able to hear over the rush of people.

He bent to examine it, but the sound only intensified, telling him they were in the last few seconds before it went off.

"What is it?" Naomi asked from behind him.

He turned, and grabbed her, using his body to shelter

hers from the blast as he threw them sideways as hard as he could.

As they fell, he swore he felt a rush of air move beside him.

"Athena," Naomi cried out over his shoulder. "*No.*"

Everything seemed to melt into slow motion.

They hit the ground and he covered Naomi with his body. At this range, there was no way he would survive the blast, but if he could block as much of the force as possible, she might have a shot.

He turned his head to see Athena, the backpack secured in her jaws, crouching low to leap. Her back legs extended, like a spring being released, and she sailed over a few other people who were huddled on the ground.

The last thing he saw was her tail, wagging as she leapt out the window.

Less than a second later, an explosion boomed, sending the whole building trembling.

Broken glass fell like rain as his heart splintered, thinking about his partner and the sacrifice she had made to save them all.

22

NAOMI

aomi screamed, tears burning her eyes.

She didn't care about the scrapes from the broken glass or her bruised hip from when Gage had thrown them to the ground.

Somehow, they were still alive because his best friend had sacrificed herself to save their lives.

The world was blurry with her tears as Gage grabbed her hand and they both scrambled up.

"It wasn't a bomb," he said to himself.

"There was an explosion," she said.

"Well, it wasn't a regular bomb, it was an electromagnetic pulse on a massive scale," he said.

"How do you know?" she asked him.

"Look at the holo-screen," he said. "Look at your bracelet."

Sure enough, the screen where news had been streaming when they arrived had gone dark. She glanced down at her bracelet to find it was dead on her wrist.

"Athena," she said.

"I know," he told her.

They ran for the lobby doors and jogged down the stairs, past the panicking crowd, and turned the corner to the side of the building.

Two dark shapes lay in the grass.

One was the remains of the backpack.

The other was a limp canine body. Its silken fur looked like a sky darkening before a storm. Heavy-looking clouds scudded across it. As they approached, she let out a soft whine.

"She's alive," Gage said, his voice almost breaking on the words. "She must have let it go before it went off."

"Smart girl," Naomi breathed.

Something darted through the sky overhead, then let out a strange hiss.

"What's that?" she asked, gazing up at the funny little metallic thing with one red eye.

"Drones," Gage yelled. "We have to go. *Now.*"

He grabbed her hand, as if to drag her to the carriage.

"Not without Athena," she said, throwing herself toward the dog with everything she had.

He was so much stronger than she was. If he had wanted to force her to leave, he could have.

Instead, he froze for an instant.

"She wouldn't leave without you," she reminded him. "She saved us."

"May the stars protect us," he hissed under his breath as he ran for his best friend.

Naomi moved to help him, but he slid his arms under the giant canine and lifted her to his chest effortlessly.

"Move, Naomi," he screamed back at her.

She sprinted for him just as something blasted the wall of the building behind her.

When she reached him, he grabbed her hand and began running for the back of the building.

"No," he murmured, stopping.

"What?" she asked.

"We can't steal a hover car," he said. "The pulse will have knocked them out."

There was another blasting sound, this one closer than before.

"The carriage," she said.

"It's a hover carriage," he told her.

"But the horses," she said. "If they're actually real, maybe—"

She didn't get to say the rest as he dragged them all back toward the front, where the carriage was parked.

A second drone had joined the first in the air. They circled above, sending out the occasional blast, ignoring everyone else.

They're here for me.

"Get them out of the harnesses," Gage yelled to her, running to the less friendly of the horses and swinging poor unconscious Athena onto its broad back.

Once the dog was settled, he moved to help Naomi. Together, they freed the horses while dodging blasts.

"We'll go back to the castle," he told her. "If anything happens to me, keep going. *Do not stop.* Do you understand?"

"G-Gage," she stammered.

"Say you understand," he yelled, his eyes flashing furiously.

"I understand," she said.

He lifted her onto her horse, and she tried to memorize the feel of his big body against hers, just in case it was the last time. She realized that their attraction was not the thing she would miss most. It was the sense of belonging, the bond that tied them together.

Please let us get through this...

He slapped her horse's flank, and it jumped forward.

She grabbed its silky mane and held on for dear life as the drones above redoubled their efforts.

The stallion ran for all it was worth, as if it knew what was at stake. She felt terrible that it was frightened of the blasts and even more awful that it was in danger because of her.

Everyone in this Center is in danger because of me.

It felt like her heart was being torn to pieces as she envisioned the huge line of employees, all of them vulnerable to the drones and whatever came next.

A moment later, she heard a second set of hoofbeats on the path.

When the trees closed in overhead, she felt a momentary relief. It would be harder to hit them in here, and harder for the drones to maneuver.

"What's happening?" she called to Gage.

"This is an invasion," he shouted. "We have to get back to the castle. It should be easier to defend."

Naomi glanced up and swore she could see a red electric eye flickering above the trees as they fled.

"If it's an invasion, why aren't there more of them?" she asked.

"The electromagnetic pulse," he replied. "Anything that was too close would have been taken out by it."

"But there are at least two here," she said.

"These two are speed scouts," he told her. "They were probably sent in right after the pulse went off. They're taking a few shots, but their main purpose is to report back and inform whoever or whatever is coming next."

"That's why they haven't hit us yet," she realized.

"Exactly," he said.

"I think I know why they're here," she told him, feeling like she wanted to throw up.

But she had to tell him. It was long past time to come clean. This wasn't how she had pictured it, but even if she died today, she didn't want to do it without having been honest with the man who would have been her mate.

"They're after you," Gage said.

She nodded.

"I guess there are a few things I don't know about you yet," he said.

"Yes," she admitted. "I'm sorry."

"When we get out of this, you will tell me everything," he said. "A mate's job is to share your troubles."

"You still want to be my mate?" she asked.

"Of course," he said, his violet eyes darkening. "Of course I do."

"I'm sorry," she said again, tears sliding down her cheeks. "I had no idea something so serious could happen."

"Don't be," he said gruffly. "I have something to share with you as well. This should put it in perspective."

She smiled through her tears, wishing she could be worthy of such a mate.

A moment later, the trees thinned, and the castle came into view.

Naomi's breath caught in her throat.

When they last saw it, the castle had been a sturdy-looking thing, constructed of massive, mossy stones and roof slates the size of mattresses. Flags had flown from the turret.

Now it was clear that the only parts of the castle that

were *real* in the way she would consider something to be real, were the parts they had been able to touch.

A moat still ran around the building, with real water in it and a wooden drawbridge, though it was a simpler contraption now. The metal ornamentation must have been projected onto it.

The big wooden front doors were there, and she could see the stone outlining the living spaces and the second floor.

Everything else was scaffolding and sheets of plain composite for hologram projection. The tower was a simple wooden platform with stone parapet Oberon must have known they might want to touch.

There were no flags, there was no moss. The castle looked like the set of a movie that planned to rely on a lot of computer effects over a green screen.

Could they really defend it?

"It's still better than being out in the open," Gage said, as if reading her thoughts.

As the hoofbeats slowed, Naomi was surprised by the almost complete lack of sound. Other than her own ragged breathing, the place was utterly silent - no birds sang, no crickets chirped, no wind whistled in the trees. And she was struck again by just how much of the place had been under Oberon's control, and how much was lacking without him.

The thought of his last words before the bomb sent a chill through her.

As long as I'm online, the Center is completely safe.

23

______

NAOMI

Naomi paced the great hall, watching Gage examine the weapons at their disposal as Athena rested on a makeshift bed nearby, drifting in and out of consciousness.

"Could be worse," Gage muttered, though whether he was talking to her or to himself, she had no clue.

The poor man probably worked in a glassy office tower every day. He had no more knowledge about this stuff than she did. Although...

She wandered over to look at the bows laid out on a wooden side table. Their shafts were a polished wood, and when she lifted one it felt like the weight was about right.

"However bad things get, we only have to hold on for about an hour," Gage told her.

"How do you know?" she asked, lifting her eyes from the bow in her hands.

"Because even in a place this big, basic security won't take more than an hour to reboot," he said with a grin, giving one of the massive swords an experimental swing.

Something about the way he moved with it set off alarm bells. He looked... at home with it.

"What did you say you do for a living again?" she asked him.

"I didn't," he told her with a frown. "Is that what you want to get into right now?"

"Is it something... illegal?" she asked carefully.

"No," he chuckled. "Definitely not."

"Then I can wait," she decided.

"Good," he said. "I'm going to start fortifying the windows and doors. Want to help?"

"Sure," she told him. "I'm pretty good with a hammer and nails."

"Looks like we're in luck," he told her, pointing to a corner of the dining room.

What had looked like a case for silver and polish when the simulation was running was now clearly a metal toolbox.

She jogged over and grabbed it, and began sorting through.

"I'll start scrapping wood for us to use," he said.

By the time she had found a nice box of vynium nails and a gravity hammer, Gage was jogging back to her with an armful of boards.

"Where did you get those?" she asked.

"Other parts of the simulations," he told her. "I figure they won't mind if they can continue to brag that no one has ever died here."

Naomi shivered and then grabbed a piece of wood from him.

"Sorry," he said. "I guess our true colors come out in an emergency situation."

"It looked like you really know how to use those swords," she said carefully.

"If only you knew how to use a bow and arrow we'd be in business," he joked.

"Archery was my favorite camp activity," she said, feeling a little pleased to surprise him. "I was thinking yesterday that it was no accident that it was supposed to be today's activity. I thought it was nice of Oberon to have us do something I'm good at. It didn't occur to me you'd be in the same position."

"I don't often use swords at work," he said.

"I don't imagine you do," she laughed, feeling a little silly. Just because he looked good with a sword didn't mean he knew how to use it.

"I mainly carry a blaster and light blade," he said, looking down at his hands. "But traditional swordplay was part of my training."

"Training for what?" she asked.

"All Maltaffians take obligatory guard training when they come of age," he told her.

"Ah," she said, thinking that sounded familiar.

She knew that Maltaffian guards were considered to be some of the best in the galaxy. Even the basic training was probably pretty useful.

"But I stuck with it," he went on. "I was the personal family guard for the Bly-Xarxyn family."

Personal family guard...

Everything began to rearrange itself in her mind. The way he treated the staff, how much more at home he was in jeans than a suit, his physical strength, his knowledge about security systems...

A Maltaffian guard?

"I'm not a wealthy man, Naomi," he continued. "I know

that isn't what you want to hear, but it's important for you to know before you make a decision about accepting me as your mate. I'm a loyal man, and I know how to work hard, but I'm just a guard. At least, I used to be."

"You lost your job?" she asked distractedly, her mind still fitting the pieces together.

"In a manner of speaking," he said, handing her another board.

She took it and began affixing it to the next window.

"Athena and I foiled a kidnapping attempt," he told her, glancing over at the dog. "Some cutthroats tried to take the Bly-Xarxyn children. We had other plans. The family rewarded us with an early retirement at full salary, and a little house. They also paid for this trip to the Center, so that I could have a child of my own."

"You and Athena are retired?" she asked. He was still so young.

"It hasn't been easy," he told her. "Athena is accustomed to going to work every day. She doesn't know what to do with herself. She's used to having a job, something to offer the world. It's like she has lost her identity."

Naomi just barely managed to hide her smile.

Obviously, it was easier for him to project his own feelings onto the dog than to open up about how he missed work himself.

"I can relate to her," she said quietly. "I'm not going to have a job to go home to either. Although in my case, it's not because I'm getting an early retirement."

She waited for him to ask what she had done.

"Did you do something illegal?" he asked, repeating her earlier concern.

"No," she said with a wry smile. "The opposite. But it doesn't matter, because we all might die because of it."

"We're not going to die today," he murmured. "Hang on."

She heard the low-pitched whine of the drone.

Gage was running for the swords, dragging one off the table to toss through the air at the thing.

He didn't hit it, but it darted away, disappearing out over the moat again.

The sword landed on the floor with a clatter.

"Keep going," he urged her. "We won't have to fight them off forever."

But she could already hear the hum of the drone again, louder this time.

24

GAGE

age grabbed Naomi and pulled her down behind the window they had just boarded up.

"It's time to stop building up our defenses, and start our offense," he murmured to her.

"What do you mean?" she whispered.

"There's enough cover here for me," he said. "But the drones will just fly in if we can't keep them away from the castle. A classic castle ground defense doesn't work when your enemy can fly."

"I'll grab a bow and some arrows and head up to the tower," Naomi said. "Maybe I can pick them off with a bit of distance, before they get to us."

"No," he said, grabbing her wrist.

"Why not?" she demanded, looking offended.

"It's not safe up there," he growled.

"Well, I hate to break it to you, but it's not safe here either," she said. "At least from there I have a chance at taking them out."

She was right, one of them had to be up there and one

down here. And he doubted she could even lift one of the swords, let alone swing it or throw it.

"Fine," he said. "The instant you run into trouble, retreat and scream for me."

"Absolutely," she said as she darted off toward the table that held the weapons.

He listened as her footsteps clattered on the stairs and then faded away. She didn't seem to be concerned about the height of the tower like she had been about the bridge. And he wasn't going to remind her of her fears. He'd seen people face down a lot in the heat of battle.

Please, let her be safe, he begged the gods.

The hum of the drones kicked up again and he headed outside to see if they were still the only enemy present.

The sky was strangely still, and he was struck by the blanket of quiet that seemed to have fallen over the Center.

Two drones darted through the air, blinking at the tower with their red eyes.

He heard a whoosh sound from above, telling him that Naomi must have loosed an arrow.

The shot hit one of the little drones, knocking it sideways in the air for a moment. It let out a series of high-pitched beeps, then righted itself.

Another arrow flew through the air, hitting the little drone again.

Its partner blasted back, and Gage hoped Naomi was ducking behind the stone parapet.

A moment later another arrow sailed through the air, this time hitting the first drone in the eye.

It let out a high-pitched sound that was almost like a scream. Smoke plumed up from it and the humming sound died as it dropped toward the ground, hitting the stone castle wall before smashing to bits on a flagstaff extending from the keep.

"Yes," Gage yelled.

Then he felt it, and knew his excitement had been premature.

The ground was vibrating slightly. Something was coming.

Gage ran back into the keep and grabbed two swords from the table, then headed back toward the drawbridge.

The bridge was still up, but now larger, ground-based attack drones were rolling closer. There were half a dozen in easy sight, but he knew there could be more hidden in the woods. It was better not to assume this was all.

Take them one by one, he could hear his combat instructor advising him in his first multiple assailant work-shop. *And if you can't do that, call for back-up before you engage. Even if it costs you time.*

Well, he had no way to comm anyone after the pulse.

But he could use the little time he had before engaging to garner as much advantage as possible.

The rolling drones were of a style Gage hadn't seen before, but he was pretty sure they weren't amphibious. And thanks to the stars, the water in the moat was real.

Each one had a blasting sphere for a "head" and a screen on its belly for gathering data about its opponent. They were probably being controlled by someone who was analyzing the data from the screens.

Squat and sturdy, they didn't look easy to knock down. He wished he had something that might catch in those treads and hang them up. But there wasn't time to scatter debris.

While he waited, he could hear Naomi loosing arrows above, trying to hit the second flying drone.

By the time one of the rollers took an experimental shot across the bridge, Naomi had felled the other drone. He heard it hit the wooden platform of the tower as he ducked to avoid the blasts.

"Nice," he yelled to her. "Stay up there. We've probably got more coming."

It was a lie.

But when the first roller slid directly into the moat water and emerged on the other side, he was glad he hadn't told the truth.

He didn't want Naomi down here in this.

"Fracking amphibians," he muttered, rushing over to slice at the roller with one of his swords.

There was a sizzling crack and the dome-blaster slid off the chassis.

He stabbed at the screen, and it cracked into smithereens, ending the feed, he hoped.

A second roller was already emerging from the water, so he went for it, repeating his slicing and stabbing and removing it from commission before it could clear its sensors of the water.

He was just beginning to feel like he had everything under control when three more emerged at once.

He spun to take the first and barely caught the second.

But the third roller had time to recover from its journey. Its dome lit up as it began blasting.

There was no time to swing at it, instead he had to try to find cover. He moved to the other side of the open draw-bridge, knowing he was still partly exposed.

Suddenly, there was a loud crash and the blasting stopped.

Naomi whooped joyfully from above and he saw that

she had dropped the little drone she had felled earlier onto the bigger one's dome.

"Nice shot," he yelled to her, sprinting back to the water to take out the last roller as soon as it emerged.

He was just turning to scan the valley to see if more were coming, when something zapped into view in front of him.

There was a shivering, bell-like sound and then every cell in his body was riddled with pain.

"That's a nerve-net," a man shouted to him from the small craft that hovered just on the other side of the moat. "I know you Maltaffians are too hung up about *universal ethics* to use them, but I find they get the job done nicely without a lot of collateral damage."

Gage sucked in a deep breath, willing himself to remove his mind from his physical reactions and stay calm in spite of the agony.

"It's a good day to die, Naomi Peterson," the man yelled out. "The sun is shining. The birds are singing."

Something about what the man said tickled Gage's pain-addled mind.

25

OBERON

Oberon awoke in darkness.

He had just spoken with Naomi and Gage, perhaps he had experienced a glitch.

And yet...

His time tracker was the first thing to blink back to him, feeding him an impossibility.

Time had passed.

Time he had not measured.

The security tasks he had been meting out carefully had all been abandoned. His network wasn't giving him feedback. There was only silence.

The AI reached out, and instead of feeling a tapestry of systems pulsing back to him in perfect harmony, he felt... nothing.

Only the clock.

And then a calendar of guest arrivals popped back into existence.

A series of messages sent between employees began to light up - all with urgent settings, checking the status of staff and guests.

And then the branches of the Center property began to reappear, each a beacon of terrible information.

The Center had been breached.

Oberon's perfect Center had been breached by intruders and his guests were in danger, but he was still not fully online and could do nothing to help.

Had he crashed? He had planned his individual system restarts so carefully to avoid it.

Feed from the security cameras began to populate and he saw a replay of the electromagnetic pulse and the brave sacrifice of Gage's canine partner.

Though it was a balm to his sense of self-sufficiency that the crash had been through no fault of his own, the idea of someone harming the Midsummer Center intentionally was so much worse.

He tried to bring up his security systems with an urgency he could only relate to the very human emotion of desperation.

But failsafes were in place, holding him back from risking another crash.

He scanned his cameras eagerly as they popped up, seeking the locations of the biological staff and guests, wondering if there would be any way in which he could help them with his limited capabilities before he fully rebooted.

Systems were returning to him faster now, a random cascade of shivering data entering his memory so rapidly he could hardly log it: the status of the candy machines in the infirmary, the water level in the decorative pond, the antici-pated life left on the ranch house roof, the updated flight pattern of the next expected client... None of it what he was looking for, but all of it was welcome, as one by one these lines connected him back to the Center, giving him a familiar sense of being anchored at a particular time and place in space. He associated this sensation of connectedness to his environs with the biological beings he served, and it renewed his sense of fellowship with them.

I will help you somehow, he promised, knowing that his promise might well be empty.

Timing was everything when it came to biological beings. They were vulnerable things, requiring a very particular set of urgent needs to be filled unceasingly if they did not wish to lose the quickening pulse of electricity that gave them life. Unlike Oberon, they could not be reanimated by a system reboot.

The situation was very grave indeed.

26

NAOMI

Naomi's blood turned to ice in her veins, and she gasped in a breath, willing herself not to panic.

On the ground below, Gage was caught in a nerve-net, according to the Intergalactic Council, such a thing was considered a barbaric form of torture. She could not imagine the pain he must be in.

Guilt crushed her heart and threatened her ability to process the situation.

He needs you to think, Naomi, not feel. Use your brain.

"Bud Bulgaro?" she guessed stupidly.

"Right on the first try," he called back sarcastically. "Why? You got more than one major crime family mad at you, sweet tits?"

"Release him, and I'll come down," she yelled.

"Don't," Gage choked out.

"No," Bulgaro sneered. "Don't bother coming down. Your boyfriend doesn't seem worth saving."

She was flying down the stairs at that, hoping an idea would occur to her by the time she reached him.

"Why?" Gage gasped.

"Why?" Bulgaro asked. "Now let's see. I could be mad at her just for working at Starling & Fleet. They charge by the fracking minute."

"Money?" Gage rasped.

"The issue for me is that her firm was hired with no expense spared, to help me develop a choice piece of land," Bulgaro stormed. "And after they took said money, she turned us in to the Intergalactic Environmental Bureau for building on land with lowland wolves."

"What?" Gage asked, as Naomi neared the bottom of the tower.

"I had a clean environmental study, which was turned in with my permit applications," Bulgaro said. "It was all cleared, until she ruined it."

"The first environmental study wasn't clean," Naomi yelled, bursting out the doors.

The wind blew her hair around her face, but she made no move to smooth it down. Nothing mattered, nothing, but saving the man she loved. Her mate.

"Of course not, sweet cheeks," Bulgaro laughed. "Why do you think I paid for a second one? For my health?"

"You bribed the second lab," she said. "You bought a faked study that wouldn't show evidence of those endangered wolves."

"Bingo," Bulgaro said. "But fake or not, that study is the one in the file. That's my land, and I can do what I want with it."

"Did you get all that, Oberon?" Gage asked, his voice suddenly sounding perfectly normal.

"I sure did," Oberon replied.

The floating craft Bulgaro stood in dropped unceremoniously to the ground.

"Hey," he screamed. "What is this? Who are you?"

"This is the Midsummer Fertility Center," Oberon said. "And I am Oberon. I am in control here."

Human and droid guards poured out of the woods and streamed for the fallen craft, more than it could possibly take to remove one furious man and cuff him.

But Naomi was already running for Gage. Instead of watching Bulgaro be dragged off while he wailed for a lawyer, she was cradling her mate in her arms.

"I'm okay," he told her. "The net was only active for a few minutes. Then Oberon came back online, and I tapped out an alert on my bracelet."

She pictured him arching and writhing in pain.

"How could you even see your bracelet?"

"I couldn't," he told her.

"Then how did you know Oberon was back online?" Naomi asked Gage.

"The birds," he said simply. "Was I right, Oberon? Are the birds and insects your way of monitoring security in open areas like this?"

"Yes," Oberon replied. "They are like nerve endings for me. I came back online and almost instantly I got the signal from your bracelet."

"Incredible," Naomi said, looking up at the sky, where Oberon's voice seemed to originate. There was a wind now, and the clouds were moving, so many signs that the Center was returning to normal.

"Just to keep the two of you up to date, both local and intergalactic forces have been notified and provided with our recording," Oberon said. "Bud Bulgaro will be in an intergalactic prison by the end of the day. You have nothing more to worry about."

But the clouds had Naomi's mind going in another direction.

"Athena," she said, leaping to her feet. "Athena is hurt."

"I scanned her immediately after deactivating the nerve net on Gage," Oberon replied. "Hospital staff is due on the scene in less than a minute to look after them both."

Relief coursed through her veins. She collapsed on the ground beside Gage and let the tears flow.

"What's wrong, my love?" he asked, wrapping his warm arms around her. "Everything is fine now. I promise. Athena is tough."

"I ruined everything," she sobbed. "All because I was afraid."

"What did you ruin?" he asked.

She thought about the Center, the castle, her law firm, her career, and everything in between.

"*Us*," she wailed, realizing it was the only part that mattered.

"Us?" he demanded, sitting up and pulling her with him.

She nodded, crying too hard to speak.

"Naomi Peterson," he said sternly. "You can ruin your clothing, your credit, even your reputation. But the one thing you can *never* ruin is us. Unless..."

"Unless what?" she sniffled, looking up into his handsome face.

"Unless my... financial situation changes things for you," he said flatly.

She was so stunned at the idea that the words jammed up in her mouth and she gaped at him like a fish.

"I would understand," he told her. "You're going to be in a precarious position. Just know that what I have will keep a roof over our heads and food in our bellies. It might not be the mountain of credits you thought I had, but if we want more, we can build it together."

The hope in his voice had tears threatening again, but she swallowed them back, knowing he needed reassurance now.

"Your financial situation sounds miraculous, Gage," she told him. "I'm so proud and amazed that you saved those children. And because of it, you and Athena have freedom most people can only dream of. And you didn't cut corners or hurt anyone to get there. Can't you see how special that is? Can't you see how special you are?"

Then she was falling into his arms, kissing him like there was no tomorrow, like she would never, ever let him go.

He wrapped his arms around her, kissing her back as if she were the most precious thing in the universe.

And that thought made her heart stutter.

She pulled back, bracing herself.

"What is it?" he asked her. "Are you afraid of the claiming? We don't have to do it tonight, not until you want it so much you can't breathe without it."

"No," she murmured. "It's not that."

"What is it?" he asked. "What else can there possibly be?"

"You know why I came here," she said, unable to meet his eyes. "You know I wasn't able to bear a child?"

"My seed will bring your womb to life," he said automatically.

"What if it doesn't?" she asked him. "There are no guarantees. What if we can never have a family?"

He pulled her close again, pressing his lips to the top of her head.

"Naomi," he said softly. "You are enough for me."

When he cupped her face in his hand, she allowed him to tilt her chin up. And she didn't care if he could see tears in her eyes again.

"The two of us will be a family," he told her, his violet eyes crinkling as he smiled down at her. "There will never be a need for more."

27

GAGE

Gage held Naomi's hand in his, waiting as patiently as he could.

Athena lay in a hospital cell in front of them, her fur rippling softly in the warm, healing gel of the cell-bed with each deep, even breath.

Other than some bad bruising and sprains, she was going to be fine. A few nights in the gel would have her back to herself in no time.

The hardworking hound was a hero all over again. Several staff members had been by to check on her already, not to mention all the hospital caregivers who had stopped in ostensibly to look at her chart, but really just wanting a glimpse of her and a chance to say a few words to Gage.

"Alright," Dr. Angoshla said, tucking her holo-board under one furry arm. "We're ready to release you, Gage."

"Thank you," he said, shooting out of his chair.

"A word of advice," she said, her eyes twinkling. "Try to take it easy, at least a little. And if you start to feel bad, don't be afraid to rest. Those nerve nets take a lot out of you. You're probably running on adrenaline."

"Yes, sure," he said, his eyes fixed on Naomi, who had risen to join him. "Adrenaline."

"I'll make sure he gets some rest," Naomi assured the Bergalian doctor.

Dr. Angoshla snorted, but she gave them a smile.

"I'll see you in a few days," she said. "And if anything changes with Athena's condition between now and then, you'll hear from me."

"Thank you, doctor," Gage said. "I'm grateful that you're willing to care for her."

"She's a hero," Dr. Angoshla said simply. "It's my privilege."

"Your suite is ready," Oberon said.

Naomi squeezed his hand, and it was all he could do not to grab her and sprint with her in whatever direction Oberon indicated.

But he didn't want to embarrass her, and he definitely didn't want Dr. Angoshla insisting that he stay in the hospital to rest.

"Thank you," he said as calmly as he could. "Want to show us the way?"

"It would be my pleasure," Oberon said.

One of the floor tiles lit up just outside the room.

Naomi gave Dr. Angoshla a little wave and then dragged Gage toward it.

He smiled at the clear sign that his mate was eager to be alone with him.

"It's essentially a very nice hotel suite," Oberon warned them as they chased the lit tiles down the hospital hallway toward a side door. "You were supposed to spend the night in the castle and there wasn't time for something new. This is a place where we house visiting VIPs."

Naomi pushed open the door and they stepped out into the night. A blanket of stars twinkled above.

Ahead of them, a lamppost pulsed more brightly than the others.

"Any place is fine, Oberon," Gage told him. "Really."

"As long as it's close," Naomi amended, pulling him toward the lamppost.

The next one began to pulse, and he gave up and jogged along with her, laughing. Her legs were so much shorter than his that it was no burden to keep up.

And he was pretty sure Dr. Angoshla was just covering her bases telling him to take it easy. He felt fine. The nerve net had only been active for a few minutes.

"Look," Naomi breathed.

He followed her eyes to a small building of about three stories, with what looked like a greenhouse on top. It was surrounded by a garden.

The lampposts pulsed all the way to the front door.

Naomi let go of his hand to sprint for the entrance, slamming her little palm against the sensor, panting and laughing at the same time.

"Easy, my mate," he teased as he jogged up to join her. "Save some of that energy for me."

But he felt the same desperate pull, in spite of everything that had happened today. His pulse pounded, and he was already so hard he hurt with his need to claim her.

The door swung open to reveal a simple living room with elegant modern furniture.

Naomi ran for the stairs and a predatory instinct kicked up in him.

He thundered after her, his feet pounding the stairs as they passed the second floor and kept going, past the third.

Naomi didn't stop until she reached the greenhouse. The

door hissed open, unleashing the lush, fertile scent of flourishing plant life.

She slipped inside and he followed, soaking in the warm, humid air as he brushed past lacy leaves and swollen blossoms, still trembling from Naomi's passage.

At last, the wild growth opened up to reveal a wooden platform holding a mattress draped in silky sheets.

Twinkling fairy lights adorned the bushes all around the bower bed, illuminating Naomi's face, which was already lit up with delight.

"This is the right place?" he asked her gently.

She nodded up at him, her eyes luminous, fingers already moving to the slide on her dress.

He watched, not daring to move, as she swept her thumb down and the dress slipped off her shoulders, pooling at her feet.

Without taking her eyes from his, she released her undergarments, wiggling out and letting them fall.

His heart threatened to pound out of his chest as she moved to him.

He was ready for her to press that delicate, bare form to his, but she attacked his clothing instead, gently touching every slide until he was wearing nothing at all.

"Naomi," he groaned. "As soon as I touch you, things are going to get very intense, very quickly. We should probably talk about what's going to happen."

"You talk," she said. "I'll listen."

She pressed her soft lips to his chest, and he felt it in every cell of his body.

Closing his eyes, he forced himself to concentrate.

"What's going to happen is called the mating frenzy," he said, through a clenched jaw, trying to ignore the sweet lips currently trailing down to his abs. "Do you know what that is?"

"No," she whispered as she knelt, her breath tickling his left hip.

"Naomi, what are you doing?" he rasped.

But it was too late, she had reached her hand out to lightly caress his throbbing cock.

The sensation lit him up from inside and he hissed in a breath. It took all he had not to wrench her hand away and bury himself in her, her mouth, her sex, any part of her would do.

"Does it hurt?" she asked softly, taking her hand away. "It's so swollen. Or does it only feel good?"

"Only feels good," he murmured, unable to yank her to her feet.

She brushed her lips against the base of him and he bit his lip.

"Naomi," he murmured warningly.

But her tongue darted out, tasting him so sweetly that he was frozen with the teasing pleasure.

Gaining confidence, she lapped up toward the tip and then swirled her tongue around it, sucking gently.

The pleasure was white hot, with a life of its own. He was already at the edge from her innocent touch, his senses raging.

With a roar, he pulled her up, lifting her in his arms and cradling her to his chest as he moved them to the bed.

28

NAOMI

Naomi fell against the silken sheets, her whole body consumed with need and shame in equal measures.

"You didn't like it," she whispered miserably.

"I loved it," he said, his voice dark with need. "So much that I couldn't let it go on. I need you, Naomi. I need to taste you, to lose myself in you, when you're ready."

She blinked back tears of gratitude.

"Would you like that, Naomi?" he whispered to her, kissing her forehead. "May I give you pleasure?"

She nodded, not trusting herself to speak.

It was clear to her that she wanted this man, that he knew how to make her body sing.

What she hadn't expected was to feel so much emotion so close to the surface - joy, shame, gratitude - all in quick succession.

And love...

Surely, she couldn't love him, after only a few days together. And certainly, he couldn't love her.

This was a mating frenzy, a physical pull.

But when she closed her eyes, he kissed her eyelids, and she saw him easing her across the bridge that first day, giving her pleasure and allowing nothing for himself, swirling her around a ballroom, and enduring the pain of the net just to keep her safe a little longer.

If that wasn't love, then what was?

He was kissing her breasts now, licking a nipple into his mouth reverently, as if it were a precious jewel.

She reached down to stroke his horns, gently at first, and then more firmly as he groaned, and his muscles tensed against her.

He fed on her breasts ravenously for another moment, then slid down to press his lips to her belly, her hips, her inner thighs, everywhere but the one place she needed him.

Need surged in Naomi, and she clenched the sheets in her fists, whining as her hips trembled.

"Yes, my love," he murmured against her opening.

Her hips lifted of their own accord, her hungry sex seeking his wicked mouth.

Instantly, he gave her what she wanted, licking her with firm, slow strokes until she was screaming with pleasure.

Gage applied himself to her with tender focus, seeming to anticipate what she craved, then pulling back just before she could fly.

"Please," she moaned, not even sure what she was asking for.

Then he was climbing up to cage her head in his arms, his eyes flashing violet and indigo as he gazed down at her.

"Gage," she murmured.

"Is this what you want?" he demanded. "Do you want to be mine forever? There will be no going back."

"Yes," she told him, afraid he wouldn't believe her. "Yes, yes, yes."

"I will try not to hurt you," he told her, his voice a sexy growl.

She waited as he took himself in his hand and pressed against her.

The size of him was frightening, but he felt so, so good.

She slid her hands up to caress his horns again and his eyes went hazy with lust.

Then he was pressing inside her, forging a path of pain that burned away to pleasure, until she was clenching his horns in her hands and jogging her hips, desperate for him to move.

With a roar of surrender, he dragged himself out and plunged back in.

The pleasure was dizzying. She cried out, losing track of herself, of everything around them.

There was only Gage, and the delicious coiling pleasure he filled her with.

When she wailed with need, he slid a big hand between them, massaging her little pearl until the pleasure shot through her and she exploded with it, feeling as if light were bursting from every pore.

As it loosened its hold on her, she could feel him tensing.

He cried out hoarsely and she felt him pour himself into her with a series of throbbing jets that went on and on.

When he fell back on the mattress at last, she crawled onto his chest, and he pulled her close, nuzzling her hair.

"Are you okay?" he asked her. "I'm sorry I lost control."

"That was wonderful," she told him honestly.

"Good," he told her. "You probably have about five minutes if you want a drink of water or something to eat."

"And then what?" she asked, surprised. She had been fully planning to snooze on his big warm chest.

"Then you'll need me again," he chuckled.

"No," she laughed.

But when he nuzzled her hair, he seemed to send sparks down her spine, and she felt the fresh hunger twisting in her.

"Ohhh," she sighed.

Then he was pulling her on top of him, feeding at her mouth as she wiggled around to find him rigid as steel again and ready for her.

29

NAOMI

Naomi awoke with light filtering in from between the palm fronds.

She stretched and felt a rainbow of soreness and pleasure. It was like she had spent a month at the gym, or like she hadn't stretched in a year.

But what had happened was neither of those things.

She and Gage had been up here so long consuming each other that she had lost track of the days.

"*Athena*," she murmured, sitting up quickly.

Gage made a groaning sound like a bear coming out of hibernation, then slipped back into sleep.

She could hardly blame him after the things he had done to her.

Flashes of him holding her against the glass to take her again and again went through her mind. The few times they had stopped for the food and water left on the landing, he had wolfed down his meal and begun feasting on her all over again while she ate, until her meal was forgotten too, and they were at it again in earnest.

She slipped out of bed, wincing as she stood from the

mattress. She really hadn't noticed how hard she was working her body. Her thighs trembled and her hips felt like they were stretched out so much they practically hummed as she walked.

The tray of food on the landing was tempting, but what she really needed was to see if Athena was alright.

When she reached the third floor, she wandered until she found a bathroom. A fluffy robe hung on the door and there were plenty of soaps and fragrant towels.

She stepped inside and closed the door.

"Oberon," she whispered. "Can you tell me how Athena is doing?"

"Good morning, Naomi Peterson," Oberon said, his quiet tone almost matching the level of her whisper. "Athena will make a full recovery. Right now, her left hip is still very sore, but she is ready to join you and Gage again when you are ready."

"That's wonderful," Naomi told Oberon, feeling relief wash over her. "I'd love to get a quick shower first, and then I can come pick her up."

"Dr. Pan will bring her to you," Oberon said. "Enjoy your shower and she'll see you when you're finished."

"Thank you," Naomi said. "I... I'm sorry for what happened. I hope being rebooted isn't painful for you, and that the work of rebuilding goes smoothly."

"I'm running nicely after the reboot," Oberon said, without answering her question. "Those normally happen only a few times per year on a schedule, so this was an unexpected boost to my efficiency. But, Naomi, rest assured that you did the right thing. You are not in control of what a criminal does in response. And I am very glad the lowland wolves will be protected. They share a remarkably similar genetic background to Athena. And she is truly a noble creature."

"She really is," Naomi agreed.

She went about her morning routine as quickly as she could, but she couldn't resist soaking under the hot water in the refresher for a nice long time. The rush of warmth soothed her aching muscles, and by the time she got out, she was feeling cozy and content.

Wrapping the fuzzy robe around herself, Naomi ventured out into the room. When she didn't see any clothing, she decided to just go down as she was. Hopefully, she could have out a bowl of water and something nice for Athena to eat before they arrived.

Her own belly growled loudly as she descended the stairs. The scent of fresh coffee and bacon wafted up to greet her.

When she reached the bottom step, she saw that Gage was already in the living room, pacing back and forth.

"Naomi," he breathed, stopping to smile up at her.

"You were sleeping so hard," she said.

"The mate bond dragged me out of bed when you left it," he chuckled. "But thanks for trying to let me sleep."

"Sorry," she said. "I needed a hot shower."

"I hurt you," he said, his face falling.

"Only in the best ways," she told him. "I feel great now."

She moved down the stairs to him and he wrapped her in his arms and nuzzled her hair.

The frenzy might have loosened its hold on them, but not enough to keep him from sliding a hand inside her robe to cup a breast and thumb the stiff nipple as he moved his mouth to hers, exploring her with a mounting excitement, as if they had never touched before.

She moaned lightly against his mouth, and he tugged

the tie of her robe loose, sliding his hand down from her breast.

But when he reached her belly, he stopped and pulled back from their kiss.

"Naomi," he whispered in an awed way, pulling open her robe and cupping her belly in his hand.

"Is it... am I?" she asked, not daring to hope.

There was no mirror in the bathroom. And he had come to know her body so well in the last few days, every inch of it...

"I think so," he told her, dropping to his knees to press his lips to her belly.

Pure joy lifted her heart, and the hope was so sweet it almost hurt.

The sound of a door clicking open barely registered with her, and she felt no shame at being half-naked in front of the doctor.

Gage rose slowly, keeping one hand curled protectively over the slightly convex shape of her belly.

"Good morning," Dr. Pan called out softly.

"Come in," Naomi said.

The doctor entered briskly. A hoverbed trailed her with Athena on top, resting like a queen on a litter.

"Athena," Naomi said, rushing over to greet the one who had been willing to sacrifice herself to save them all. "I'm so glad to see you."

Athena turned to her and butted her head against Naomi's shoulder in greeting.

Naomi stroked the soft, cloudy fur in wonder. Were they finally friends?

"She didn't forget that you refused to leave her," Gage said. "You proved yourself on the battlefield, and you have her respect."

He strode over next, and the normally regal Athena turned puppyish, wagging her tail, ears down in happy submission as they greeted each other.

"She'll need rest and plenty of good food," Dr. Pan said. "And she's been spoiled *a lot* by the staff, so she's expecting attention. But in a few more days, she'll be as good as new."

"We can do all of that," Naomi said. "No problem. We're so grateful to all of you for taking good care of her."

"If I'm not mistaken, someone else here may need special care," Dr. Pan said, her eyes twinkling. "Let's get your vitals."

This time, Naomi was eager for the exam.

"Where are your thoughts today?" Dr. Pan asked as she pulled up the sequence on her bracelet.

"All good things," Naomi said, smiling over at Gage. "I'm feeling hopeful."

"Good," Dr. Pan said, smiling and placing the sensor.

"Temperature is normal," Dr. Pan said. "Heart rate is normal, blood sugar normal, blood pressure normal."

Her fingers danced in the air as the hologram shifted and flashed.

"Are you in any pain right now?" she asked.

"No, uh, unexpected pain," Naomi said.

Dr. Pan's eyes flicked up to hers.

"I'm just a little sore," Naomi confided quietly. "But it's a good sore, from consensual things."

Dr. Pan nodded and looked like she was trying not to smile.

"I have wonderful news," she told them at last.

Gage moved to Naomi's side, wrapping an arm around her shoulders as Dr. Pan removed the sensor.

"You are expecting," Dr. Pan said.

Naomi barely managed not to scream with excitement.

Gage pressed his lips to her hair and squeezed her tight.

"Maltaffian pregnancies are notoriously fast," Dr. Pan warned them. "Usually not more than a week or two from start to finish."

"A week," Naomi echoed.

"You'll want to eat as much as you can," Dr. Pan said. "It won't be hard. You'll crave food constantly. Just obey the cravings."

"Yes," Naomi said, suddenly feeling almost faint with hunger.

"Make sure she has everything she wants and needs," Dr. Pan said, turning to Gage. "You'll stay here until the birth, so we can assist you with everything. But it's your job to be alert and listen to her."

"It is my honor to help in any way I can," Gage said.

"I think I smell breakfast," Dr. Pan said with a smile. "That's a good start."

"Would you like to join us?" Gage offered.

"I have another visit to take care of this morning," she told them. "But thank you for the offer. Oberon is with you day and night, and I can be here anytime. Just let him know if you need me."

"Congratulations to you," Oberon said softly.

"Thank you both," Naomi said, meaning it with all her heart. "This feels like a happy dream."

The lights in the room glowed a little brighter for a moment.

Then Dr. Pan gave them a friendly wave and headed out the door.

"Breakfast time, little mate," Gage said to Naomi.

"Not without Athena," she said, heading over to the hover bed and sliding her fingers along the sensors to program it to follow her bracelet.

Athena leaned over and gave her casual lick on the cheek.

"I can see someone has a new best friend."

Gage's tone was teasing, but he looked so happy that it made Naomi's heart throb.

30

NAOMI

A few days later, Naomi sat by the edge of the pool, with Gage rubbing her swollen feet.

Her belly was growing so swiftly that she just found it easier to spend most of her time naked. Dr. Pan had assured them that making love would not harm the baby. With her in a perpetual state of undress, and Gage constantly by her side, they were happily riding out the tail end of the mating frenzy.

The obvious joy he took in caring for her seemed to light him up from within like a star.

Gage had just lowered his mouth to nuzzle her thighs when she sensed Athena waking up beside her.

If Gage was her sun and moon, then Athena was her shadow. Naomi had tended to the recovering canine just as Gage tended to her.

Now the two were inseparable.

Athena head-butted Naomi's side and let out a low whine.

"Do you need a job?" Naomi guessed.

The cool water of the pool felt good to Naomi's swollen body. And it was an excellent place for Athena to heal.

She grabbed one of the rubber balls she kept nearby and threw it into the water.

An instant later, Athena launched herself into the air, her cloudy fur turning cerulean blue as she arched herself down into the water and swam for the ball while Naomi cheered her on.

Athena scrambled out of the water and shook herself off, sending a spray of water everywhere.

Naomi laughed, and then felt a tightening around her belly.

Her hands went to her middle.

"Naomi?" Gage murmured.

"I think it's time," she told him.

"Oberon," he bellowed frantically.

"Everything is fine," Oberon said. "Dr. Pan is on her way."

"Where do you want to be?" Gage asked Naomi.

But her midsection was tightening again, and this time it hurt.

"I don't think there's time to go anywhere," she told him when it eased a little.

"The lounger," he said, pointing to the long, cozy chair by the pool.

"Yes," she gasped as her middle tightened again and a fresh wave of pain washed over her. "It's happening so fast."

"That's normal for Maltaffians," he told her as he lifted her gently and carried her to the chair. He sat, lowering her down between his legs so that she could lie back against his chest.

In seconds, Dr. Pan was jogging in with two helpers. They began examining Naomi, while Gage ran his fingers through her hair and told her how brave and beautiful she was.

The words were soothing, but the pain intensified with each contraction.

"We can't give you anything," Dr. Pan said sympathetically. "But that's because you're going to be a mom before it would have a chance to kick in. Are you ready to meet your son or daughter?"

"Yes," Naomi gasped.

"Then push," Dr. Pan said with a big smile.

Thankfully, the agony of her labor was short, just like the rest of the pregnancy. After only a few pushes, there was a feeling of release, and the miraculous sound of a baby's cries.

"Oh," Naomi sighed.

"You have a beautiful, healthy daughter," Dr. Pan said happily.

"Leandra," Gage said, his voice tinged with wonder.

"That's a lovely name," Dr. Pan said as she briskly wiped down the little one.

"It means lion-girl," Gage said. "We hope she will grow up to be as fierce and brave as her name."

Leandra let out a growly cry and Naomi laughed as tears leaked from the corners of her eyes.

At last, her daughter was bundled in a cotton blanket and tucked into her arms.

"Hello," Naomi whispered, gazing down at the beautiful little face.

Leandra was the same pale green as her father, with tiny horn nubs on top of her head. And she had dark eyes and a little fluff of dark hair on her head, just like her mother.

Her small green hand caught onto Naomi's finger and each gazed at the other in wonder.

The staff quietly disappeared, leaving the family of three holding each other close.

Naomi closed her eyes and tried to memorize the sweet joy she felt, with her daughter in her arms and her mate wrapped around her.

A cold, wet snout at her thigh reminded her it wasn't just the three of them.

"Hey, Athena," Naomi said softly. "What does my best friend think of my daughter?"

Athena sniffed at the baby's blanket, a solemn expression in her lovely eyes. After a moment, she lay down at Naomi's feet, not in the sprawled-out way she had begun napping in after her injury, or in the curled-up ball she favored at the foot of their bed at night, but in a symmetrical and ready position, like a sphinx.

"That's her work position," Gage murmured. "She considers herself on duty now."

"Wow," Naomi said.

"Just a warning that she adores kids," Gage chuckled. "She might be someone else's shadow now."

"Our best friendship was short-lived," Naomi said with a wry smile.

"That's okay, my mate," Gage murmured, nuzzling her hair. "You'll always have me."

She let her head fall back against his warm chest and soaked in the feeling of family. She was right where she was supposed to be.

"Forever," she whispered to him.

"Forever and ever," he promised.

***

Thanks for reading **Naomi**!

Want to read Gage and Naomi's **SPECIAL BONUS EPILOGUE**? Sign up for my newsletter here (or just enter your email if you're already signed up!): www.tashablack.com/bonus-naomi

About the next book:

Are you ready to find out what's going on with Naomi's bestie, Chloe, in the next book from the **Alien Surrogate Agency?**

Check it out now:

Chloe: Alien Surrogate Agency #5

Tashablack.com/aliensurrogateagency.html

TASHA BLACK STARTER LIBRARY

Packed with steamy shifters, mischievous magic, alien adventures, billionaire superheroes, and plenty of HEAT, the Tasha Black Starter Library is the perfect way to dive into Tasha's unique brand of Romance with Bite! Get your FREE books now at tashablack.com!

ABOUT THE AUTHOR

Tasha Black lives in a big old Victorian in a tiny college town. She loves reading anything she can get her hands on, writing sci fi and paranormal romance, and sipping pumpkin spice lattes.

Get all the latest info, and claim your FREE Tasha Black Starter Library at www.TashaBlack.com

Plus you'll get the chance for sneak peeks of upcoming titles and other cool stuff!

Keep in touch...
www.tashablack.com
authortashablack@gmail.com

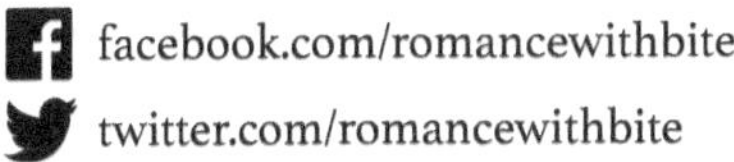

facebook.com/romancewithbite
twitter.com/romancewithbite